Sicilian Dynasty

Daniela Di Benedetto

Translated by Elizabeth Fraser

T0159402

Trinacria Editions
New York

ISBN 9780991588619

Part 1

Antonio's Diary (1965-1985)

July 18th, 1965

Today, the black and white cow gave birth to a calf. I delivered it myself: what an unforgettable day!

Papa was in the vineyard, keeping an eye on the farmhands, when the cow went into labour. I just happened to be passing in front of the stall when I heard her groans, so I rushed off to find Papa, and God only knows how long I spent running round the vineyard trying to find him. There are times when I wish that we had less land: it's so easy to get lost.

"Hell," said Papa when he heard the news, "it's already sunset, it'll be dark before we find the vet."

"Why?" I asked. "There's no need to call the vet. I'll help you."

"No, I'm tired. Tell your brother to get the car and go and look for Pino."

"Alfredo's reading in his room. Please Papa, we can deliver it ourselves. I know what to do. I've been there every time the vet's come."

"Alfredo's reading? Why? He got his diploma a week ago. He should be burning those books instead of reading them!"

"Leave him be," I said. "We don't need him. Let's go."

"You keep out of it. It's no job for a boy."

"How much do you want to bet that I can't do it? And if I win? What will you give me if I win?"

"Well, if the cow dies, you'll get a beating...."

In the end I convinced him, but he wanted Nunzio there to give us a hand, not only because he keeps cows and therefore has a lot of experience, but also because Nunzio is the closest of all our neighbours — it took me ten minutes on my motorbike to get him. I only asked him to come to keep Papa happy, and actually he didn't do anything for that cow; it was I who delivered the calf while he just stood there and watched!

Obviously Papa knew that I would have managed. I might be only fifteen years old, but I've already learnt all there is to know about running a farm. I'm sure that Papa wishes that Alfredo were like me. He's always moaning because my brother isn't interested in neither animals nor plants. I love Papa and I usually agree with him about everything, but when it comes to Alfredo, he doesn't see him like I do. Alfredo is a genius, and although he hasn't got the countryside in his heart like we have, he's good at so many other things. He left high school with the highest grades, while I didn't even bother with high school. When Papa dies, Alfredo and I will get the farm, and I'm sure he'll know more than me about the financial side of the business, the taxes to pay and those kinds of things. Who says we don't need an intellectual in the family?

July 19th

Still, there are times when my beloved brother really annoys me. He was sitting there reading when I told him. I would have expected a little enthusiasm on his part. But no...

"I delivered it myself," I said. "Don't you want to see it?"

"I'll see it tomorrow."

"What are you reading that's so interesting?"

"The Civil Code," he replied. "The laws that govern private property."

"What do you care about all that stuff?"

"There's a trial starting tomorrow. Caruso versus Turdo. I want to go and watch. It's of interest for everybody in the agricultural community. It could happen to us, you know — one of our goats or cows could wander off into one of the neighbour's fields and start grazing there."

"I don't think Nunzio would ever take us to court for that."

"It's got nothing to do with how litigious your neighbour is. It's the principle that counts. Who's going to pay compensation for the damage caused?"

"If you really want to go to court tomorrow, I'll come with you."

"You'll be bored out of your mind."

"I'm never bored when I'm with you."

He smiled. I said it on purpose so that I would see that irresistible smile with the dimples.

Who knows if he loves me as much as I love him. Sometimes I think that it suits him to have me around, just because my dull personality makes his shine all the brighter. When we get together with our friends, all the girls crowd around him to hear his jokes, but I'm always the first to laugh to show the others how funny he is. I give his ego a boost, but what's wrong with that? The girls would follow him even if he weren't funny because he's just so handsome, as handsome as a movie star. He gets his looks from Mama, whom Papa married even though she didn't have a dowry because her bright blue eyes turned heads wherever she went.

It's odd that despite being chased by loads of girls, Alfredo, at nineteen, has never had a girlfriend. If he had, he would have told me. And anyway, I would have noticed if something had been going on. But he doesn't even look at the girls in our group. Maybe he doesn't want a girl from country stock, but a girl like Kim Novak, the fabulous blonde in *Vertigo*. He's covered all of the walls in our room with photographs of her, and everywhere I look I see those feline eyes staring back at me. I wouldn't want to marry such a beautiful girl; I'd be worried that the others would want to take her away from me. But Alfredo shouldn't be worried. There aren't any men who could hold a candle to him, so he can get away with dreaming of a Hollywood star.

It's a shame that he hasn't fallen in love with Nunzio's daughter, Tina. We grew up together, and when we were small, I was sure that sooner or later she would have become my sister-in-law, and Papa also thought the same thing, but now I think that something's changing. Yes, that damned high school diploma's gone straight to his head. Perhaps he thinks he's better than all our old friends. It really annoyed me when he continued reading that stupid book while I was telling him about the calf....and I told him:

"You've changed."

"Why do you say that?"

"You used to play with me. You used to enjoy bullfighting with the calves too, and you used to go horse riding with me and with Assuntina. But now all you do is stay in your room and read. It was fine when you had to study, but now the exams finished."

"Oh Antonio, get a grip. I'm nineteen years old and I'm too old to play. One day, you too will have to grow up."

"You're never too old to spend time outside and go riding. And anyway, it's good for your health."

"If Tina comes round tomorrow, we'll all go riding together, okay?"

Who knows if he'll keep his promise...

Yesterday evening I discovered that Papa thinks the same way about Tina. We've always been telepathic.

After dinner, while Mama cleared the table and Alfredo had already gone back to his room, I heard Papa mutter, "I'll never understand that boy. Now that his exams are over it wouldn't hurt him to spend some time with Tina. How are they supposed to fall in love if they never see each other?"

"Leave him alone," replied Mama. "Why are you trying to force them together? Alfredo can get a girlfriend who's much prettier than Tina, and richer. She's got two sisters and two brothers. I don't think she'll get much land. A little something for her dowry they'll give her, and that's all."

The conversation was getting interesting, and I wanted my parents to feel free to continue their discussion in private, so I pretended to go upstairs, but in fact I stayed on the stairs to listen. I had always suspected that Papa wanted Alfredo to marry Tina, not only because we could have added her land to ours, but also because of the close friendship he has with Nunzio. Tina's sixteen now — maybe it's a bit early to think about it — but there'll be trouble if somebody else were to ask for her hand before Alfredo. I don't think my mother's convinced though. She wouldn't think a princess worthy of her favourite son. I know that she loves him more than me, but I'm not envious, I've got Papa.

"What's wrong," Papa asked, "with wanting the daughter of my great friend as a daughter-in-law? If Alfredo doesn't want her, I would be happy for Antonio to take her instead."

I was right to stay and listen! He would never have said that in front of me. Cunning, eh? Marrying me off like that.

"Antonio?" exclaimed Mama. "He can marry whoever he likes! Alfredo's got to find a wife first."

She's right. My brother's older than me.

"So far, Alfredo hasn't had a single girlfriend," Papa muttered. "He's the type to think and think about it, before finally getting married at forty. I really do hope that at least Antonio will marry young. Otherwise I'll die without seeing my grandchildren."

"I doubt he'll marry young," replied my mother. "As long as Alfredo isn't married, he'll carry on thinking that all the women belong to his brother."

She's right. My mother has never shown me much affection, but she's always right.

We had to postpone the horse ride because this morning all of us went to the courthouse to hear the trial between Caruso and Turdo. It's such a stupid case. The farmer Caruso has accused his neighbour, the shepherd Turdo, of not watching his goats, as they often wander onto Caruso's land, nibbling on the new shoots and causing untold damage. As Turdo doesn't give a damn about Caruso's land, Caruso has started to confiscate the goats he finds saying that he would keep them in lieu of compensation. And that's when the lawyers got involved.

I don't know why my brother is so interested, but Tina's interested because Caruso's her uncle, her mother's brother. That's why we were all in court this morning.

To be honest, I only went because Alfredo was going but then I hoped that there would be a fight between the two parties and I would get to see it, but Alfredo told me that neither party can insult the other side — otherwise they would get fined by the judge. We had to sit through the reading of lots of legal stuff which was really boring so I passed the time trying to make Tina laugh.

"Look," I said, "the Picciotto sisters are here. Obviously they'll want to know what's going on. Their plot of land is so big that a dog has to stand on his hind legs to pee."

"Shush. I want to hear what the lawyer's saying about my uncle."

"Ah, so you like the lawyer do you? He's a handsome man, but you've got competition. The younger Picciotto sister is staring adoringly at him. Who'd have thought? Even old sticks have feelings."

"Stop it Antonio, or I'll have you kicked out of the courtroom."

Damn. Now even *she* has become serious.

During the break, Alfredo started talking to a man I don't know, someone he'd met there. They talked about the law and it sounded as though my brother knew the Civil Code by heart. It was incredible. I was a bit jealous because he wasn't talking to me, but there's no way I could've taken part in their conversation. I tried again with Tina, but she didn't want to know.

"Why did you come?" she asked. "You're not interested in what's going on. You haven't listened to a word."

"I thought it would be more entertaining."

"You're a child," she replied, so full of disdain it was as if she really wanted to hurt me. She thinks she can talk to me like that just because she's a year older than me, does she? Well she can go to hell! I wasn't going to let her ruin my day.

Rather it was Alfredo who ruined it for me. We were at the exit. He was moaning because the sentence was unjust, the judge had ruled that Caruso must give the goats back to Turdo and that Turdo must pay a small sum as compensation for the damage caused, but according to Alfredo, the sum was too low.

"The judge doesn't understand the first thing about cultivation," said my brother. "He has no idea about the amount of damage a goat can do by eating the new shoots. Caruso should have been awarded a lot more money. Or maybe the

7

judge understands perfectly and is in cahoots with Turdo."

"Come on," I said, "there's no point getting pissed off over something that's got nothing to do with us! Why are you so bothered?"

"Because these kinds of dirty tricks are only played in Sicily. When I'm a lawyer, I'm going to send all the corrupt judges to prison."

"I stared at him wide-eyed. "When you're a lawyer?"

He changed the subject immediately. "Let's go. I promised you that I would go horse riding with you and Tina. You still want to go, don't you?"

"Of course." I let the lawyer comment drop. But I'm worried.

July 21st

Today we had a good ride out on the horses. These are the only moments when I think that Tina really is beautiful, with her blonde hair blowing in the wind, her nostrils flared out by the smells of the countryside, her cheeks red from the exertion. She isn't sexy like Kim Novak, but she has a good body for a horsewoman, and when she's riding she seems to be nature incarnate, so different from that stand-offish young woman in court with all those airs and graces. She's sixteen years old — a difficult age for a female. There are times when she is a girl and times when she is a woman. She knows how to cook, I've tasted the dishes she prepared, and it seems as if she's ready to find herself a husband; but I still can't forget that when we were five or six years old we used to play together, and we would take a break to pee under the tree! Who knows what face she would make if I reminded her.

After she had gone, elegant and lithe on her horse, I talked to my brother about her.

"Isn't Assuntina lovely, Alfredo."

"I know she's lovely, it's not as if I've only just met her."

"Do you want to marry her when you're older?"

I shouldn't have said anything, he was almost angry with me: "Great. As if Papa wasn't enough, now you've got the same idea."

"But I've always thought that, that you would have ended up together."

"Just because we grew up together?" replied Alfredo. "No. I'm not in love with her."

"Do you like someone else?"

"No. It's too early to think about all that."

"Anyway, I'm sorry you don't want Tina. She's basically part of the family."

"If that's the case, why don't you marry her?"

"I'm a year younger than she is. She looks down on me. I might never get married. I don't trust women. They're fickle. On Monday, they'll say one thing and on Tuesday, the opposite."

Alfredo laughed. "I would say that we've got to know them well enough!" he said, pinching me under the chin. It's his way of caressing me.

I love that caress.

July 22nd

I heard Mama and Papa arguing again today. Papa was complaining because Alfredo reads too much, and she was defending him.

"You've never understood the importance of learning," said Mama, "weren't you expelled from school because you threw a jar of ink at the math teacher?"

I didn't know that. I had to swallow my laughter since I didn't want to be discovered.

"Who told you that?" muttered Papa.

"Your sister Maria told me, she's older than you. You're not calling her a liar are you? Anyway, with or without the jar of ink, you didn't even finish middle school."

"So what? What would have changed? Even if I had graduated with a degree in agriculture, I couldn't have made my farm any better, or any richer, than it already is."

"In that respect, I can't criticise you. If you'd studied though, you would have more interesting friends. The people that come round might have been less boring. Do you really think that I enjoy having to talk to donna Franca and donna Michelina, who only talk about their recipes or what their grandchildren have been up to?"

I'm learning loads of interesting things by eavesdropping! I would never have thought that my mother wasn't satisfied with her friends. Now that I think about it, she was poor when she married Papa, but her family were more cultured. She had left school in the last year of high school and was a pretty good piano player. Her brothers were accountants. Papa courting Mama was accepted because of the wealth of the farm, but Papa was a rough farm boy, like me. That's why she favours Alfredo, the only intellectual in the family.

"So your friends aren't good enough for you anymore?" said Papa. "Are you sure that you would have more fun if you changed your environment? I'd like to see you among the ladies of high society! Do you know what they talk about? Designer clothes, nail polish, the slut who cheated on her husband. I doubt they are more interesting than donna Franca and donna Michelina. It's all female chit-chat."

Papa's right. He may be ignorant but he's not stupid, and he knows that Mama's not stupid either.

Female chit-chat! It's so difficult to find conversation topics that a woman likes. Alfredo manages to entertain all the girls by making them laugh. But I'm not as clever as he is, and when I'm alone with Tina I never know what to say to her so we end up sitting there in silence.

She's always in a bad mood when Alfredo's not around. Maybe she's in love with him. Who knows? We've made so many plans without once asking ourselves what Tina thought.

I'm worried that Alfredo will spend less and less time with us. They were good times back then, when Alfredo was fifteen and I was eleven! Once Papa beat us because we had been playing at bullfighting with a calf who was just starting to sprout horns. I would do it all again, beating included, to see the Alfredo of those times once more.

I want my brother back. But he's in his room, flicking through old books.

August 3rd

It's boiling hot. Actually, here in the countryside at least you can breathe a little; in the city, it's hell. Never in a million years would it cross my mind to get in the car and drive the fifty kilometres to Palermo on a day like today, but Alfredo did. He went to the courts to listen to a trial for an honour killing. Who gives a damn?

August 4th

Something terrible happened at lunch. Everything started with an argument between Alfredo and Papa. Papa wanted to use the car this morning to take a farmhand, who had hurt his hand, to hospital, but the car wasn't there because Alfredo had taken it to the courthouse. Papa had to make do with the van which is a lot slower, and at table he exploded at my brother for taking the car for something that wasn't important, and asked him what the hell he was doing at the courts anyway.

To which Alfredo had replied: "I'm interested in these cases because I'm going to be a lawyer."

Mama and I, we didn't move a muscle, we just looked at each other. I had expected Papa to tip the table over, but he stayed calm and replied: "You know full well that you will inherit with your brother two hundred hectares of land and that your future lies here."

"Listen Papa," Alfredo responded, "Antonio can manage on his own. I'm not cut out for this type of work. Why can't you just let me go?"

"Are you saying that you want to give up your part of the inheritance?"

"Yes, if you give me some money to pay for my studies, I'll relinquish everything else. I'll even put it in writing: 'all the land shall go to Antonio.'"

"You're free to get a degree, if that's what you want, but in agriculture. That's the only degree you'll need."

"No Papa, I want to be a lawyer. It's my calling."

"Do you think it'll be fun spending all your time in a dark and dusty courtroom?"

"Anything's better than in a barn," replied Alfredo. That's the last thing he should have said. Papa was furious.

"You wretch!" he shouted. "How dare you turn your nose up at all that I, my father, and my grandfather lived for..."

"No Papa, I'm sorry, I wasn't turning my nose up at anything, it's just that there are those who are born to do something, and there are those who are born to do something else…"

"I'll tell you what you were born to do. To help your brother here. He knows the difference between a healthy cow and a sick one, and you've had the fortune to have been given the gift of a superior intelligence. You know how to distinguish between a good deal and a bad deal, to keep the accounts. Together, you two can take this farm to great heights."

"I'm sorry Papa, but my plans are different from yours."

I'd never seen Alfredo so pale, tense, so decidedly against Papa. I kept quiet because hearing their words made me want to cry. Mama was silent too, she seemed shocked.

"And now," continued my father, "pack your bags and leave my house. You're legally an adult so I won't come looking for you. But you won't have a penny from me for your university studies. I don't want a lawyer in my house."

"No problem," replied Alfredo, "seeing that I want to study in Bologna."

His final words woke my mother up, and she let out a moan. Certainly, if her son wanted to become somebody that was fine by her, but so far away, no! That horrified me too. Alfredo in Bologna! I wanted to scream while Alfredo explained to my father that the best law programme in Italy was in Bologna, and that he didn't want to become a small time lawyer forced to work for peanuts, but famous, and after graduation he wanted to come back to Sicily to fight the Mafia. I'd never heard him talk like that before. Fight the Mafia! Alfredo seemed to me to be the type of person who only thought about himself, but is he actually an idealist? I'm bitter because I thought I knew my brother, but after listening to him talk, I don't think I know anything about him. He never confided in me, never talked about his ambitions! Our friendship must have meant nothing to him.

He was arguing his first case: Papa versus Alfredo. And he finished by saying that Papa shouldn't worry, because I would give him all the satisfaction that he needed. Me!

"You're just using your brother," said Papa. "Now tell me this and I want the truth: If you didn't have a brother, if these lands didn't have other owners, would you have abandoned them to follow your stupid calling? Would you have sold them?

Answer me: Would you have sold the lands of your ancestors?"

"No. Selling terrain that turns in a healthy profit never makes good business sense. I would have rented them to a tenant farmer. But I've got a brother, so it's never going to be an issue. And anyway, I would never refuse to give him advice if he were to ask me."

Papa calmed down a bit when he heard those words. But only a bit.

"Don't ever come running to me for help," he said eventually. "Go to your mother and your brother, the fools who have given you all sorts of ideas, treating you like a god, and who you now want to abandon along with this farm. Why don't we ask them what they think?"

Mama's face was white. She stuttered, "I don't know, I didn't expect..."

She really didn't know what to say, but Papa was pitiless: "You can't, can you? You can't defend him. And you were so happy when he spent his days reading books about law instead of helping me keep an eye on the fields. Antonio, why don't you say anything? He wants to leave you on your own with the weight of this huge farm on your shoulders. Haven't you got anything to say?"

Well, what could I say? I was annoyed with Alfredo for not having told me about his plans for the future, but then there were those words, *when I am a lawyer,* and I understood. Something had, slowly and painfully, been worming its way into my conscience for some months now: Alfredo isn't like us; he wasn't born to live in the country. It was inevitable that sooner or later he would leave, to become a lawyer or something else that had nothing to do with our farm. It's just that I'm not ready to let him go yet. It's happening too soon, too quickly, and when Papa asked me to join in, I thought that if I opened my mouth I would cry. So I didn't say anything.

"You're on your own," said my father. "Not even your adoring followers support you. Do as you wish. If you decide to go to Bologna, you'll get there by hitchhiking, and you won't have a lira from me in your pocket."

Poor Alfredo. I'm sure he thought that he could have counted on me and Mama, but we just sat there, silent. He looked at us, bewildered, then he got up from the table and went to his room. I felt as though I had betrayed him.

I was overcome by remorse, so I went to join him. He looked at me as though he expected me to abuse him too, but all I said was: "Why didn't you tell me?"

There was a sadness in his eyes that I had never seen before. "I was scared of your reaction. Papa's. Mama's. Everybody's. It wasn't easy to talk about it. I was forced to tell him. Didn't you see what a disaster it was?"

Yes, brother, I understand. I'm left with no choice but to forgive him. He was sat at his desk with his head in his hands, desperate, and then suddenly he said: "Antonio, help me!"

It was the last thing I expected to hear. "Me? What can I do?"

"You've got to convince Papa that you're happy to take on all of the land, that you'll manage on your own, and you've got to convince him to give me a bit of money. He'll listen to you. He doesn't really want to make me hitchhike to Bologna and wash dishes in a restaurant to pay for my studies!"

"Bologna! I've got to help you leave me forever?"

"No, only the four years of university, then I'll come back. This is where I want to practice."

"That's as long as the lure of the north doesn't make you change your mind. I've heard lots of stories of people who leave Sicily and never come back. They say that it's more civilised up north. Why don't you just go to the university in Palermo?"

"Ahah... So you agree with Papa! How could I ever have thought that country folk would understand." There he stopped himself, aware that he had insulted us, aware I was looking at him with the eyes of a wounded animal. "Very well, I'll go to Bologna and I'll wash dishes or worse, just to earn some money, but I'll go anyway. And if you don't help me, you'll never see me again."

Then something incredible happened: I saw tears in his eyes. I'd never seen him cry before, never; I didn't think he could. I felt really bad, and I understood that I had been selfish, and that my brother's happiness was more important than mine.

"Alfredo, please —" I started, but he no longer thought that I would help him, and interrupted me saying, "Get out. Leave me alone, get out."

But rather than leave, I sat down. It's my room too; he had no right to kick me out.

"Alfredo, listen to me. I'll help you. I'll sell the scooter that Papa bought me, I'll go and sell it tomorrow so that I'll be able to give you the money for the trip." What else could I give him? I've got nothing else.

Immediately his face changed. I could tell that he appreciated my offer. "You would do that for me? You're very sweet, but it won't be enough. I'll be there for four years."

"I'll talk to Papa, I'll do everything I can. Just like you asked me to."

Then Alfredo hugged me. He held me tight and I had to fight the urge to cry.

"When are you leaving?" I asked.

"At the beginning of September. When the university opens."

"You will write to us, won't you? You'll write every week?"

"Of course I will."

I could have stayed in his arms for the rest of my life.

August 6th

Last night, I had just fallen asleep with my head on Alfredo's shoulder, when we were awoken by our mother. It was midnight when she came into our room and started to gently stroke my brother's shoulder.

"I've brought you my savings," she said. "Your father doesn't know, you'll need them for your trip." She held the bank notes out to him, but he was still half asleep; he probably thought he was dreaming.

"Oh, Mama..."

"Now you can go without having to worry about anything. I'll send money to Bologna every month, even if I have to steal it from your father."

She too was able to make sacrifices, and this time Alfredo's embrace was for her. I withdrew into a corner of the bed, like a puppy who thinks that his space is being invaded. I'm so stupid: I was jealous. But not for my mother's love for Alfredo.

September 3rd

He's gone. Not hitchhiking, but by train, first class. Papa was the only one who didn't want to come with us to the station, all the rest were there: me, Mama, even our neighbours Nunzio and Tina. When the moment came to say goodbye, Alfredo didn't get upset, actually he was radiant with happiness. It'll have been because he had got what he wanted. Mama, however just stood there, as stiff as a marble statue: she would never have admitted that her favourite son had hurt her. Tina seemed rather indifferent when he gave her a brotherly kiss on the cheek. Then he said goodbye to me, with the usual rough caress under my chin, because he's convinced that men shouldn't kiss one another. But that caress made me want to scream.

Now that I'm finally on my own, I can cry. I'm alone in my room, which was also his, looking at Alfredo's bed which is now empty, looking at the photos of Kim Novak that cover the walls which I would never dare take down even if I couldn't bear them. The room reverberates with Alfredo even though he is not here. How will I survive?

How will I be able to bear being apart from him for so long? Four years, and that's assuming that he graduates on time. Three hundred and sixty five days multiplied by four. An eternity. It's best not to think about it.

I tried to take my mind off things by going for a walk, but the countryside no longer smells the same, the bleating of the lambs sounds like a lament. All that I used to do with Alfredo bores me now.

For some reason I can think of loads of funny jokes that he entertained me with for years. Like the Hamlet parody: "to be or not to be? That is the question. Whether 'tis nobler to suffer the bites of a hostile bedbug or to take arms, crushing them and putting up with the smell…."

I'm such an idiot! I'm destroying myself with memories as if Alfredo were dead. But he'll be back and he will make us die laughing again. I must remind him to compose the second verse of the Ballad of the Old Picciotto Sisters. It's still not finished.

I can't understand how Tina can be so nonchalant; she enjoyed herself in his company as much as anybody did. This afternoon she asked me if I would go horse riding with her, and Alfredo had only left this morning! Amazing! I felt as if someone had broken the silence at a wake by asking for a cookie. I said that I didn't feel like riding, but she insisted: "Why? Summer's almost over, let's make the most of the good

18

weather."

"I've got a headache," I replied, but she didn't believe me.

"You've got nostalgia, that's what. You should learn to live without your brother. You're old enough now."

Papa had said something along those lines too, but I'm not ready to accept a lecture from Tina yet!

She's only a year older than me, but she's already distancing herself from my world, just like Alfredo did. I'm losing another friend, and this made me lash out at her and I said: "You couldn't care less that he's gone. I bet you've got plenty more boys lined up."

She looked bewildered for a moment, and then she understood what I meant and replied: "Alfredo wasn't mine. But neither was he yours. He belonged to himself. Antonio, try to grow up, otherwise you'll end up the only child in a world of adults."

She left immediately after that — thank goodness she went. I wanted to slap her. I never want to see her again.

She doesn't love Alfredo and I don't want to see her again.

June 1966

I think the letter that Alfredo sent us this week was very reassuring. This is what it said:

"Dear All,

I'm pleased to be able to tell you that my third exam has also gone extremely well: highest marks again. I'm going to relax for a week and then I'll come and see you all, if Papa's not still angry with me. But it won't be a problem if I have to spend the holidays in Bologna: the student who shares my room loves a good party and always invites loads of girls. Don't worry: I won't get any of them into trouble. I wouldn't let anything delay my graduation.

Neither should you worry that I'm living in a hellhole: these girls aren't whores. They study, graduate, and then go to work. But they rarely become housewives, like they are in the south; those who don't study become factory workers, which I think is fantastic.

Love to you all, even that curmudgeon Papa, Alfredo."

September 1967

A letter's arrived that I don't like:

"Dear All,

There's no point filling you in on all the good grades I've been getting. I'm sure I'll graduate on time and will be back in Sicily within two years. I can take my professional exams in Palermo.

I will be sorry to leave Bologna, I'm fond of this place and I've made great friends. I'm studying with a fellow student called Arianna, a beautiful girl and frighteningly intelligent. She's living proof that not only women with manly faces and bodies like barrels study law!"

It's the first time that a girl has caught Alfredo's eye. I hope there's nothing going on between them other than studying.

October 1968

I've written to my brother:

"Dear Alfredo,

I'm counting the days that divide us. I'm feeling more and more lonely now that Tina has left. She's got married and moved to the city: would you believe it, married at nineteen! Why would such a beautiful girl decide to take on certain responsibilities? She could have enjoyed life in the country for a little bit longer, the countryside, the horse rides... Her brothers and sisters are too young to be friends with me. Did you know that her mother had another baby after you left? They called her Eva and she's beautiful, blonde like Tina, but while Tina's got a large nose, Eva's got a pretty little doll's nose. Other than that, I've got nothing new to tell you. Papa's suffering from rheumatism and I help him a lot around the farm, at least it keeps me occupied.

Your letters haven't mentioned your fellow student Arianna: why? Is it because you're not interested any more? Or is it because you're very interested? Either way, I'm curious. Write to me."

June 29th, 1969

A letter from Alfredo:

"Dear All,

I'm the happiest man alive. I graduated with top marks, although I'm sure none of you are surprised, but I've also got some news for you: I'm married.

You must forgive me for not telling you about my intentions to marry Arianna: I would have preferred to wait; I wanted to be an established lawyer and be earning lots of money before thinking about a wedding. But then I realised that I was about to leave Bologna and I would have lost Arianna for good if I hadn't asked her to marry me there and then. How could I expect her to remain in Bologna and wait for me for goodness knows how long, while I tried to find work in Palermo! She's so beautiful that another man would have swooped in and flown off with her! I'm so crazy about her, I threw caution to the wind and married her immediately, and who cares that we haven't got any money. We are coming to Palermo together and we'll both look for work. I'm sure Papa hasn't forgiven me yet, so I won't ask you to put us up, but I'll need somewhere to stay. I hope Antonio will start looking for a house for us with reasonable rent right away; my wife and I will come once the house has been found.

Love, Alfredo."

Married! Married to a woman that we don't know anything about! Why would he do such a thing? If he really didn't want Tina, he could have married another girl who lives nearby, one of the many who hang onto his every word. And having a wealth of memories in common would have made our youth last longer. I'm not very good at expressing myself, but what I mean is that if I were to see Alfredo together with one of our old childhood friends, I would have felt happy to spend time with them. But he has married a stranger. I hate her.

"I'm crazy about her," he wrote but those words chilled me. What sort of witchcraft did this woman use to turn my well-balanced brother "crazy", my brother who had always considered girls to be nothing more than decorative, an appreciative audience for his jokes? He's "crazy about her," crazy enough to marry her without a job, without money, without a proper ceremony, *without us!* My Alfredo would never have done something like that. She must have changed him. He won't have any time for me when he comes home. And he had the audacity to ask me to look for a house for him! I won't do it. He can stay in Bologna for all I care. He's dead to me now.

Obviously, Arianna will look like Kim Novak. She's always been Alfredo's idol, her photos are still staring down at me from the walls. They have become the symbol of my brother's absence. For four years they have waited for his return. But now I think that Kim Novak's eyes are mocking me. I hate her too. I hate all women.

July 5th

A letter from my mother to Alfredo:

"My Dear Son,

There's no need for you to look for a house. After four years, your father has finally decided that a lawyer in the family could be useful, and he isn't angry with you anymore. We want you here. You and your wife will live with us, our house is big enough for everybody, and for your future children too. Come home as soon as possible, I can't wait to meet Arianna.

Love, Mama."

She's making the best of a bad situation. I'm sure that she doesn't approve of this marriage either, but he'll never know. She's an impenetrable woman, I've never been as close to her as I am to Papa, but something's clear: she who loves Alfredo, who encouraged his career, and who gave him the money to leave, could never, ever complain about the consequence of those four years in Bologna because Papa would say "it's your fault." Oddly enough, the person who is the least upset about this marriage is Papa. If you consider that he doesn't give a damn about Alfredo, it's not surprising that he doesn't care who his wife is, as long as she's not a bad sort, and my brother would never marry one of those.

In my head however, Arianna is a slut. Today, I did something really strange: I looked long and hard at the photos of Kim Novak, almost as if I wanted to get used to the idea that this is what the ideal woman looks like…. Then I got some coloured pencils and defaced the photos by drawing really heavy make up around the eyes and on the lips. I wanted the diva to look like a prostitute, the most vulgar prostitute in the world. I don't know why.

July 20th

They've arrived. They certainly chose a good day for travelling: it was swelteringly hot. At the train station I could barely tolerate the heat and then the train was late, which made me more nervous than I thought I would be.

When the newlyweds finally got off the train, the first thing I looked for was Alfredo's face, afraid that I would find him different. Well, something had changed: his features had hardened slightly, and he'd grown a short black beard. Now he has the beauty of a man, not a boy.

His elegant cream suit, his tie, his perfectly creased trousers caught me off guard… I'd never seen him dressed like that before. Lawyer. *Lawyer.* That word took up all the space in my head and I wasn't able to think of anything else; it was as if there was a stranger standing in front of me. I gave just a fleeting glance at his wife: brunette, slender, medium height. She looks nothing like Kim Novak. Have my brother's tastes also changed?

First he hugged Papa and Mama, then he turned towards me. "Hey, Antonio! Haven't you got anything to say to me?"

"Your beard" was the first word on my lips. "The beard makes you look older than you really are. Promise me that you'll shave it off."

He started to laugh and pinched me under the chin: the same old caress It was only then that I recognised my brother, and all the old emotions resurfaced again. I felt like screaming.

"The beard?" he replied. "You and Adrianna have the same tastes, she asked me to get rid of it too. Okay then, seeing as it's two against one: you'll both get your wish."

Arianna. I finally looked at her face and she's not bad, although she's no Kim Novak. A small nose, small chin, small mouth. Everything's small except for the eyes. Two huge eyes of intense blue made even more so by her raven black hair.

Let me introduce you to the new Signora Altavilla, "said Alfredo. "Don't just stand there. Kiss the bride."

I must admit that we weren't very welcoming: Mama only said "hello," and Papa, not wanting to repeat what Mama had said, muttered, "beautiful girl." They kissed coldly and I had to kiss her too.

What did I expect? That she would be wrapped in a cloud of oriental perfume? She didn't smell of anything. The only thing I noticed was her softness, far softer than any face I had ever kissed. Obviously her skin had never been exposed to the sun. That's Bologna for you!

I just said "Hi," but she spoke to me kindly. "Hello, Antonio, your brother hasn't stopped talking about you."

She had a beautiful voice. Low and velvety. If she sang, she

25

would be a contralto. What has Alfredo said about me?

I continued to look at the faces of the newlyweds while they argued over their luggage. My parents and I had driven to the station in Papa's car, thinking that there would be enough room for all five of us on the return journey, but we had forgotten about their suitcases. We're not talking about the usual two suitcases. Alfredo only had one, but that woman had three, plus endless bags.

"Oh Christ!" cried Mama. "What have you brought with you?"

"Nothing." said Alfredo. "Don't forget that my wife is from Bologna. She had to bring everything with her, even her books."

Right, her books. I'd almost forgotten that she too was a lawyer.

Eventually the bride and bridegroom decided to follow us in a taxi, and they went off with their tons of luggage. I watched them go, jealous of the ease with which she lent on Alfredo's arm, as if he were her man, only hers, forever! Who did she think she was?

Beautiful, cultured, distinguished, well educated…I should have known. The perfect Alfredo would never have chosen an imperfect woman. They'll be a model couple…or will they? If Arianna doesn't make him happy, I'll scoop out her eyes.

I'm being selfish, wicked. Why am I being like this? Why am I so spiteful towards a woman who's never done anything to hurt me?

I tried to atone for my wicked thoughts while we were on our way home in the car, my parents and I, all of us morose. Then my mother said suddenly: "She'll be pregnant, for sure. My son would never have married with such haste otherwise, without telling me, without inviting us to the reception. She's got to be pregnant."

So I replied, "Mama, don't be ridiculous. Didn't you see how flat her stomach was? I doubt she even weighs fifty kilos."

My mother stared at me with a mocking glint in her eyes.

"You had a good look then."

"Yes, Mama, and I hate her. We're in for an interesting summer."

July 22nd

Mama says that we've got to save face with the neighbours, we can't let them think that we don't like Arianna. Therefore we have to throw a party to welcome home Alfredo and his new bride.

Mama's organising everything, it will be the first flash of colour in the grey life she lived when Alfredo was away. I think she's doing it to show the neighbours the bride's flat stomach in her evening dress so that nobody could think badly of her, like she did.

Alfredo, however, is too intelligent to not understand that Mama's not happy about Arianna being here. He says that as soon as he's earning enough, he'll buy himself a house, but who knows how many years that will take, but in the meantime he needs something to lighten the mood. Naturally, he thought of me. It's not the first time that he has come to me when it suits him.

This morning he came to find me in the stables while I was milking a cow, a job that, in theory, I should leave to the farmhands, but I've always liked milking. Alfredo came over, saying cheerfully: "Hey, you're getting really good at that!"

He had completely ignored me for the past two days, so I didn't feel like saying anything nice.

"Take care not to dirty your suit in this stall, lawyer."

His face darkened. "Antonio, are you angry with me?"

"No, sorry. It was only a joke."

"Don't you start! My wife and I will be forced to sleep at the local doss house if you start mocking me too."

"I told you I was joking. Did you want to talk to me?"

"I only wanted to ask you what you thought of Arianna."

"Nothing, I replied - seeing that I don't know her yet."

"You'll get to know her. She's intelligent, sensitive, and… it's not for me to list her strengths, but I'm afraid that Mama and Papa will never grow to like her. They've had it in for her from the start."

"What are you on about? Get to the point."

"I'm getting there. I'd like you to treat her, not with kindness, but with affection. I want you to love her as much as you love me. Is it too much to ask?"

For a moment I thought that Alfredo had already guessed that I was jealous. "Why are you asking me?"

"Because Papa is a piece of ice, and Mama's smiles are false, which is worse. I would like my wife to not feel uncomfortable here. I would like at least one person to be genuinely nice."

"I see."

"I've got to get back to the books. I've got exams coming up and Arianna might feel neglected. You're the only one I can trust to be there for her when I'm busy."

"You know full well that I don't know how to entertain a woman."

"I'm not asking you to entertain her, just to show her a bit of warmth. Take her around the farm with you, show her how we live here, show her the animals. She might grow to love this place."

"Why should she love it? You don't love it and you're planning to leave as soon as possible."

There must have been a hardness to my voice which wasn't lost on Alfredo. He threw me a disappointed look. "Well," he said "maybe I have asked too much of you. I'm sorry for disturbing you."

He was about to leave the stall when I called him back. I'm not capable of parting from him while there is bad feeling between us.

"Alfredo, wait!"

He turned to look at me. Hope rendered his eyes even more beautiful.

"I'll do what you want me to do. I'll do my best. I promise."

I found the idea of scampering round the farm with that outsider repugnant, but Alfredo's smile was reward enough. I needed that smile.

July 24th

The party was last night. But I, despite my promise to Alfredo, couldn't cope with hearing the sugary compliments paid to the newlyweds by the guests. I don't know why, but seeing the couple smiling irritated me, so I pretended to have a headache and retreated to my room.

I thought that no one would give a damn about my presence at the party, and that no one would have come looking for me. But it was Arianna who came and knocked on my door!

"Antonio, come down," she said, coming into the room. "The guests are asking for you."

"Don't you think it's odd that they're asking after me? After all it's *your* party."

"It's everyone's party. The brother of the groom has to be there. What are you doing up here?"

"Forgive me, I've got a headache…" Then I remembered the promise I made to Alfredo and I was ashamed of my lie. "I've taken an aspirin. I'm waiting for it to take effect. As soon as I can feel it working, I'll be down, okay?" I thought my reply would have made Arianna leave, but instead of going, she sat on the bed that my brother slept in when he was a bachelor. "Antonio," she said sweetly, "Is there something wrong?"

How did she know?

"Arianna, you mustn't think for one minute that your presence annoys me, or something like that."

"Okay, but you're obviously upset about something. Why can't you think of me as your sister and tell me the truth?"

Treat that stranger like a sister…well, that is what Alfredo wanted me to do. I couldn't send her away.

"It's just that …. I haven't seen Alfredo for four years. I think he's changed."

"Changed? How?"

"I don't know. If I were to describe the boy that I knew, you would see that it isn't the same man that you married."

"Really? Give me an example."

"He was only concerned with enjoying himself, and making sure the others had a good time too. Has he ever told you about *The Spinster Saga?*"

"No. What is it?"

"It's a type of poem that he composed inspired by two spinsters who live on the farm next door. It started like this:

They were two abominable ladies,
Who were neither rich, nor great beauties.
One had the face of a hideous hag,
The other dressed like the worst kind of slag,
Wore her skirt so terribly high,
Showed the world her knobbly thigh,
And the hair upon her head,
Was a lovely shade of bloody red!"

Arianna stifled a laugh. "Did Alfredo really write that? Tell me the rest!"

"Oh, I can't remember all the verses. Hang on, there was one in the middle that went something like this:

Then one day, word got round,
That one of the sisters a suitor had found,
A pirate captain, if truth be told,
Who wrote her sweet nothings and sent her gold,
But seeing her face gave him such a fright,
That he disappeared off into the night.
Caught the mail train that left at three,
The last we heard, he was back at sea!"

At this point she was howling with laughter and I felt strangely excited. It was the first time that I had made a woman laugh, even if it was with someone else's jokes. She's beautiful when she laughs. Her eyes, her hair, even her teeth sparkle.

"That's cruel, if those ladies really do exist," she said.

"It's not as if he sang it under their window!"

"And now you think that Alfredo is no longer capable of having fun?"

"He's still capable, he just hasn't got the time anymore."

At last I understood why I was so sad and I felt a weight lift off my shoulders.

"I understand," murmured Arianna. "I understand what you're trying to tell me."

"Really?"

"You're caught up in the past while Alfredo is moving away into the future. It's no one's fault. It's just the passing of time."

"It's true."

"And it will be time that'll cure you of this sadness."

No, I should have said. *No, Arianna, time can heal everyone but not me. You don't know what Alfredo meant to me, nobody knows.*

31

"I'm going downstairs," she said, getting up. "They'll be looking for me everywhere."

"Okay. I'll be down in ten minutes."

"I'll be waiting for you." She left the room in a rustle of silk.

I don't hate her anymore. I can't. I can't find anything wrong with her. She's a good person — no one would have left their own reception for ten minutes to look for a sulky lad like me.

I could have cried. And then I really would have had a headache. I forced myself to go downstairs.

Arianna and Alfredo, shoulder to shoulder, came over to me, smiling. Evidently they had talked about me.

"Antonio!" cried my brother, "Did you think that this party was the right moment to talk about *The Spinster Saga?* You really don't want to grow up, do you!"

"But there was so much tenderness in his words that it couldn't have been a rebuke. Arianna was still sniggering."

"Alfredo, please don't ever introduce me to those ladies. I wouldn't be able to keep a straight face! How did the rest of the poem go?"

"If I remember correctly, in every verse there was a fleeing boyfriend, one on the six o'clock train, one on the seven o'clock, because it rhymed," he said.

"And the last fled on the ten o'clock?"

"No, it was an open poem. You could add other verses."

"Don't you think now is a good moment to finish it?" asked Arianna.

"Yes. Poor donna Zina Picciotto, what do you think about marrying her off?"

"Marry her off?"

"In the poem obviously." Alfredo thought for a second and then started:

"One of the sisters found a beau,

An ambassador from Mexico.
Caught him while he was rather squiffy,
Thought to marry him in a jiffy,
What a shock when he saw his wife,
He was out the door in a thrice,
But at the station he waited in vain,
The station chief had cancelled the train!"

Arianna howled with laughter. "Oh Alfredo, you're priceless!"

Yes, he's priceless. I don't know how he manages to invent them so easily. But although I really wanted to hear the end of that poem, I just couldn't laugh. I knew that last verse had also closed a chapter in his life.

August 20th

Times are hard for Alfredo. He has to study for his bar exams while trying to find a work placement in a lawyer's office. He hasn't got any time for anyone, but I'm keeping my promise. I'm dedicating myself to Arianna.

I don't know how interested she is in the things I show her. I don't think she really gives a fig about the names I've given to the calves, or when the threshing season is. Maybe she just pretends to be interested to be polite. But this morning she asked me to teach her how to ride, and at first I said that I didn't want the responsibility as her body is so delicate; if she breaks her back, my brother will want my head.

"Please!" she insisted, "I'm an adult, and I'll take full responsibility if I fall. A good ride out on the horses will make the time pass more quickly."

"Are you bored of living in the country?"

"No, August bores me. Everybody's on holiday and

everything stops. It'll be completely different in winter as I'll be out looking for work."

"What kind of work?"

"I've got a degree in law, but I'm not cut out to be a lawyer. I could teach law, or find a job in an office. That's what I thought I would do before I met Alfredo, and then I said to myself, Palermo or Bologna, same difference. One job is as good as the next."

"Does Alfredo know?"

"Of course he knows! Why? Do you think he would be against me getting a job? It suits him too. We could do with another wage coming in. Sooner or later we'll have our own house and children, we'll need the money."

That's the kind of woman she is — a woman like all the others, who wants economic security and a couple of kids. I had thought that Alfredo would only like extraordinary women, but the only thing extraordinary about her is her beauty. She just wants a normal, boring life.

I'll teach her to ride a horse.

September 10th

She's already learnt! She's become the perfect horsewoman in record time. She reminds me of Tina. It's a shame that she's not Tina, and that she's not a countrywoman. She considers it to be only a bit of summer fun; her real dream is to shut herself away in an office! What a waste!

She's got long hair, and when the wind messes it up, she shakes her head, making it tumble down one side of her face. Her hair is too black; on a colour so dark, the first white hairs will really stand out. I try to imagine what she will be like in twenty years time, with her hair peppered with silver, but then I think that she comes from the north, and women from the north dye their hair the minute they see the first white strands. My mother would never do such a thing.

Anyway, I've got a beautiful sister-in-law, and I must admit that Alfredo made a good choice, even if I did expect the mirror image of Kim Novak.

It's strange: he's never asked me what happened to all those photos. I would have found it difficult to explain how I disfigured them, so when I heard that the newly weds were on their way, I threw them away.

I don't think that my brother really cares about the things he used to love when he was a boy anymore.

September 20th

Today war broke out. Arianna had been into town to buy the newspapers for the job vacancies, and that evening at the table she talked to Alfredo about a possible job opportunity. This made Mama's ears prick up.

"What vacancy? You're not thinking of going out to work are you?"

"Why not?"

"A girl who has just got married has to raise her children."

"All the better," said Arianna. "When I'm pregnant and when I've got a newborn to feed, I'll get paid leave. That's the law, Mama."

"But what will happen when the child's two or three years old, and your maternity leave runs out, who will look after it then?"

"If I'm working, I will be able to pay a babysitter."

"An outsider? That's not how it works here."

"Well, where I come from, that's what we do," retorted Arianna, "and there are people who do the same here in the south too. We aren't in the Middle Ages any more."

"With 'here,' I meant in the houses where a sense of family is still important."

"I'm sorry to disappoint you Mama Elena, but I'm going to find work. Alfredo and I can't take advantage of your hospitality forever."

Let the battle commence! My mother is far too authoritarian; I like it when someone dares to challenge her. It seems like Arianna is like Alfredo: nothing can stop her once she's made up her mind.

Mama then turned to Alfredo. "Alfredo, haven't you got anything to say to her?"

"My wife is free to do as she wishes."

Mama didn't want to show how angry she was, especially since the couple in front of her were so calm. All she said was: "Don't count on my help to look after your children. So many young people think that's what grandparents are there for."

"Mama Elena, no one's going to ask you to do anything," replied Arianna, and this is when I stepped in:

"If you're going to have a baby, I'll look after it."

I earned grateful looks from the newly weds and an angry glare from my mother for my trouble.

After lunch I accompanied Arianna on a ride and I really do think that it'll be the last of the summer; it's September 20 and the weather's changing. It was cloudy today, and I was about to give up on the idea of going out, but my sister-in-law said: "Let's go, I want to enjoy the last day of the holidays. Tomorrow I've got to start preparing my job applications."

I find it difficult to stomach the idea that those damned books would take yet another friend away from me.

"What kind of marriage do you two have?" I grumbled during the ride, "Alfredo is more interested in his studies than he is in you, and now you want to bury yourself in your books too. It's supposed to be your honeymoon."

36

"We've had our honeymoon, and it went on for quite long enough."

"It won't be easy for you here. Alfredo will dedicate himself to his career, and my mother will do everything she can to make life difficult for you."

"Don't you think I already know that?" She said it almost as if I were the troublemaker. "I don't understand," she said. "You defended me at lunch."

"And I'll continue defending you for as long as I can. I was only asking whether you will ever be happy here."

Arianna smiled. "I'm used to fighting. I've had to fight against my parents too – they didn't want to me to marry a Sicilian."

"Oh." That surprised me. Who wouldn't want Alfredo for a son in law? "I don't know anything about your parents. What do they do? What are they like?"

"Both are government employees, and both are adorable. I was sorry to fall out with them over this."

"Was it worth it?"

"What do you mean?"

"Don't you miss your parents and your city?"

"When you fall in love everything else comes second. Didn't you know that Antonio? Have you never been love?"

"No. But one thing's for sure, I would never leave my home for a woman."

She smiled again. "I don't regret anything. Alfredo has something that makes you leave everything and follow him. But you would never understand. You're not a woman!"

I do understand though. I know what she means. Nothing beats sharing a room with Alfredo, his smell, his caresses, to be on the receiving end of a kind word or a smile. He was mine before he was hers.

Alfredo has something that makes you leave everything and follow

37

him. Her words upset me but I didn't want her to know, so I changed the subject.

"I can feel the odd drop of rain. We'd better turn back."

"Okay."

The storm caught up with us halfway home, so we took refuge in an old tool shed. She shook out her wet hair and rolled up her sleeves and didn't utter word of complaint: thank goodness she wasn't one of those silly city geese that are terrified of catching a cold the minute a raindrop falls on their head.

I watched her. Her wet shirt clung to her breasts; she was so beautiful and I was an idiot. Alfredo had asked me to make sure that she felt at home here and all I've done is tell her a load of rubbish.

I'll never know how to behave with a woman.

February 25th, 1970

Great news: Alfredo has become a lawyer and has already won his first two cases. Arianna has passed the written exam for the post office, and just today she told everyone that she was pregnant. I'm sure it wasn't a coincidence. She and Alfredo must have planned to have their first child as soon as they were more secure financially. I could never imagine my brother experiencing anything without having planned it first.

Good. The child will be fun for me too. It's too cold to work much and I'm going out of my mind with boredom. Spending hours in front of the window looking at the rain depresses me. Why? A real farmer should never get depressed over something as trivial as rain; it's part of nature.

Having said that, this morning I cried over the death of an old cow. That's not a normal.

I'm bored of riding on my own. Arianna's as round as a barrel so she can't come with me. She says that the baby will be born sometime between the fifth and tenth of November. Luckily, her oral exam for the post office position is a month before she's due and she's able to study a lot at the moment, now that she has to stay inside and rest. They say that those who get taken on will start on the second of January next year. Arianna will go in for a few days before taking maternity leave to look after the baby, which will be two months old. It's all sorted, but my mother isn't happy. She's still annoyed because she's convinced that Arianna should stay at home and be a housewife. She's been ignoring her daughter-in-law and not showing the slightest interest in her pregnancy. It's always me who brings Arianna a glass of water, or picks her books up off the floor.

Not even Alfredo is as attentive as me. He cares about her, but if for example, she asks him to buy her a pair of socks, he'll forget because he's so busy with his work. I've told my sister-in-law to ask me to do her errands for her. I'd do anything for her and as my reward I sometimes get a smile of thanks off Alfredo. He comes back from the office dead tired and hardly smiles at anyone.

I can't wait for the baby to be born: maybe, when the baby's here, my brother will stay at home for a little bit longer!

I was so jealous of Arianna, but I'm not jealous of the baby because seeing that his parents won't often be at home, I'll be able to bring him up how I want. I'll teach him how to love the countryside!

It would be a perfect baby if it takes after Alfredo physically, but has my character and loves me as if I were his father! I'll give it everything that Alfredo has taken away from me.

November 7th

Little Fabio is here! He's healthy and beautiful, he's got Arianna's blue eyes, but I'm not as happy as I thought I would be.

Even those curmudgeons the grandparents have softened, and now everyone wants to cuddle the baby. There's always someone ready to take him and I only get to cuddle him every now and then.

I wish he were mine, only mine.

November 10th

Today I'm happy because Arianna has asked me to be a godfather at the christening! She hasn't got any brothers and there aren't any other young people in the family, so she chose Tina and me. Actually Papa chose Tina, but no one could think of a reason why she shouldn't be a godmother.

My old playmate will be an absent godmother as she has her own children. This means that Fabio is mine. This time, he's really mine.

June 14th, 1971

My nephew gets more and more handsome every day. I often look after him and I've learnt everything there is to know about how to give him his milk and how to change him. Arianna's gone back to work and hired a babysitter, but she can't always be there. Today, for example, as I was coming home after shearing the sheep, I found the girl on the front doorstep with the baby in her arms and an angry look on her face.

"They haven't come home yet," she said to me, " neither

your brother nor your sister-in-law, and my time is up!"

"Don't worry," I told her. "Give me my nephew, I'll prepare his milk."

When Alfredo returned home, Fabio was in my arms peacefully sucking on his bottle. I met my brother's gaze hoping for a smile of thanks, but he was so tired that all he did was mutter "hello."

"Everything okay in the office?" I asked.

"Yes. Excuse me, I've got to prepare the notes for the closing statements tomorrow."

He withdrew into his study. After a quarter of an hour, Arianna arrived and she looked just as tired as he did. But her face lit up when she saw me with the baby in my arms.

"Oh, did you give him his milk?"

"It's a pleasure, you know it is."

"You're a star," she said, taking Fabio from my arms. A star. I wish Alfredo had called me that.

"Is my husband home?"

"Yes, he's in his study. He said he has to prepare the notes for the closing statements tomorrow."

"I should go in and help him."

"Why should you?"

"Didn't you know that when he finishes writing the outline of a speech, I'm the one who types up his illegible notes?"

"No. But you look worn out. Your eyes are red!"

"It doesn't matter. I enjoy myself doing it."

How I understand you Arianna. My wonderful Alfredo, the devourer of souls. Our only purpose in life is to help him get what he wants.

Perhaps his ungratefulness makes you as unhappy as it makes me. Now I know I can love you as if you were my sister, because you belong to Alfredo, you're part of him. You're the sister I never had.

41

Today I'm worried. I remember the day that Alfredo told us he wanted to become a lawyer very clearly: it wasn't just a way to earn money. He wanted to fight the Mafia.

Now that he's involved in a real Mafia case, I'm worried about him. His sense of justice has driven him to defend a young twenty something called Vincenzo Collura, who, while he is no angel, risks being imprisoned for a murder he didn't commit. His family have been involved in a bloody feud with the Messina family for years, and the Messinas have decided to use the youngest Collura as a scapegoat for the murder of one of their boys. Only my brother knows the truth: that Collura isn't a murderer, but he doesn't want everyone to know what he was really doing when the Messina murder took place. The evening in question, he was setting a neighbour's trees alight as a punishment for not paying protection money! I've already said that he's hardly an angel, and by admitting to something like that, he would get a prison sentence anyway. But if a witness swears that he saw, with his own eyes, Vincenzo Collura near the car where Messina's body was found, then that witness is lying; even worse, he's been paid to frame the lad.

My brother knows that the witness, Calogero Sardo, is an enemy of the Collura family: twenty years ago, he was accused of having killed one of Vincenzo's uncles, but was cleared due to lack of evidence. Understandably Alfredo wants to build his defence on the unreliability of the witness, but Sardo was acquitted twenty years ago and has been clean ever since, and no one remembers that old story anymore. Alfredo's going to bring it back into the public eye again. After receiving a tip off from Vincenzo's parents He went to get the files from the archives at the courts, and he'll ruin Sardo's reputation — he now runs a garage — surprising him with this story during the final hearing. Whether it's a surprise or not, someone knows what my brother's doing and I'm scared. These people are dangerous.

November 5th

I was right to be worried. Tomorrow is the final hearing in the Collura trial, and Alfredo has received an anonymous threatening letter. He didn't want us relatives to know: the letter arrived at his offices and he put it in his pocket and returned home, without saying a word to anybody. He was agitated however, and when Arianna asked him "Is something wrong?" he replied "All good," and made a sign as if to say "I'll tell you later." Only his wife knows everything. Someone in his family has to know so they'll know what to do should something happen to him. How I wish I were his confidant.

After dinner, I did something terrible: I waited until Alfredo and his wife had gone back up to their room and then I went to listen outside their door. I heard whispers: the letter didn't contain any clear threats, only "leave Sardo alone" or something like that. However everyone knows they are murderers.

Arianna should have had hysterics and begged her husband to walk away! But she was calm and collected, murmuring suggestions as to what to do, tell the police, tell the judge, pretend to be ill so that the trial will have to be postponed. Then Alfredo said in a slightly louder voice: "Pretend you're ill, you shouldn't leave the house for a bit. I wouldn't want them to carry out any reprisals against you. It would be so easy to throw some acid into your face while you were leaving the post office."

His words made my blood run cold. Alfredo knows the risks he's taking, why doesn't he just stop? What would happen if they were to kill him?

"I'm off to the study," I heard him say. " I'll prepare my notes and make a few calls, with the door closed so that my family won't be able to hear me."

She, as calm as always: "What time will you come to bed?"

"I don't know."

"Do you need help with the notes?"

"No, darling. Not tonight."

"Okay. I'll be waiting for you. It doesn't matter what time you come to bed I will be awake."

It could be the last time that they make love! And she knew, for Christ's sake, she should have been throwing herself at her husband's feet.

I was about to let out a cry of desperation when I heard Alfredo moving towards the door so I hid in a dark corner on the landing. I saw him go downstairs and head towards his study, but I thought that I should speak to Arianna before talking to him. It was absurd that a wife who loves her husband doesn't try to stop her husband from getting himself killed.

I knocked and she opened the door immediately. We stared at each other and I was shocked to see that the woman who had spoken so coldly only a couple of seconds before, was trying to hide the fact that she was crying: she was betrayed by her eyes which were still glistening. She was just as amazed to see me.

"Antonio? It's late. What do you want?"

"You've got to stop him! I cried, "Arianna, only you can stop him!"

I watched as it slowly dawned on her that I knew everything. But she was a rational creature: rather than waste time denying the truth or to reprimand me for having eavesdropped, she took my arm and dragged me into her room, closing the door after me so my parents wouldn't hear.

"You will never be able to stop him, "she replied. "It's

useless even trying."

"Why don't you remind him that the day after tomorrow, his son turns one and risks being left an orphan?"

"It wouldn't help. His ambition and his pride come before everything, even before his family."

"I don't believe you. If you won't beg him to stop, I will," I said.

"You can try if you want to. He won't listen to you. I know what he's like. I would love him more if he turned his back on his principles, but I would respect him less."

"Don't talk rubbish."

"It's the truth. I knew he was a decisive type when I met him, and I'm just like him. I don't know whether we would have got married if we hadn't been so similar. We share the same values, and what he expects from his wife is…that she is capable of rising to the occasion when it is required of her." She was trying hard to stop herself from crying, she was suffering, but her words in that moment, revealed the person she really was. My brave, proud Arianna — the female version of Alfredo. That was why I managed in such a short time to overcome my initial jealousy and to love her.

"Okay," I said. "I'll go downstairs and talk to him. I'm not his wife, he won't be expecting heroics from me."

My sister-in-law smiled at me through her tears, opened the door, and gently pushed me out of the room saying:

"Good luck."

It was only when I was on the landing did I realise that I was upset, sweaty, my heart thumping, and not only because I had to face Alfredo. Something strange had happened: I had seen Arianna in tears for the first time and I had an erection.

I didn't know that something so disgusting could happen. My brother was risking his life, my sister-in-law was in hell, and seeing her cry excited me, and….I wanted to throw her down on the bed and have her. What kind of monster had I become?

I remembered my first real erection when I was twelve years old. It was when Alfredo brought me a porn magazine and explained a few things to me, and I felt the heat rise and didn't know what was happening to me…my brother started laughing but continued with his explanations. The little I do know about sex, I learnt from him. But why now?

It's not the right time to think about such silliness. I've got to talk to Alfredo.

I've already waited outside his study door and I heard him on the telephone but I didn't want to interrupt him. I'll wait until he finishes his conversation then go and knock. It's one in the morning but how will I ever be able to sleep?

November 5th, evening

I wish it were all a nightmare! I wish I could fall asleep and wake up tomorrow and discover that none of this had ever happened! I talked to Alfredo. I started off calmly by asking him to change his defence so as not to discredit Sardo. His reply:

"Change my defence? In other words, I've got to persuade my client to admit that on the night of the crime he was setting fire to don Ciccio Levantino's trees? Of course it would be easy, don Ciccio would come and give evidence and my client would be sentenced to five years in prison rather than life! And he deserves to be. But that isn't the point, Antonio. The point is that I want to send the Messina family to prison: they are the worst people I have ever met. Especially Vincenzo, the victim's younger brother. I'm convinced he was the one that killed his brother, and do you know why? So that he would inherit all of his father's money. If the victim really had been killed by a stranger, Vincenzo Messina would be off looking for the real killer instead of blaming poor Collura."

"But if Collura's cleared," I said, "it would mean that Messina will be charged."

"This is where the threats I received come into play. I've informed a lot of people, I'll be under armed guard so it'll be very difficult for them to kill me. Let them try! If they do, the judge will issue an arrest warrant against the Messina clan. Do you realise that if everyone had the courage to do what I'm doing, the Mafia's power would be weakened?"

My childhood hero! Now I can admire him for something much more than his feats of bravery and his intelligence. There he stands, the author of *The Spinster Saga,* ready to die for his principles. But however much I admire his stance, I could never accept the risks. "Alfredo," I stuttered, "don't scare us to death, don't bait the Mafia. Think of me."

That was the wrong think to say and I corrected myself immediately: "Think of all those who can't do without you! Think about your son and Arianna."

"Now that you've mentioned her name, let's talk about her. I can rely you, can't I? I mean, in the worst case scenario, should something terrible happen to me. Mama and Papà have never accepted my wife, I brought her into a hostile environment and I haven't given her all that she deserves, because I haven't had time. You're the only one who cared about her. Will you protect her? Promise me you'll protect her. You'll look after her and the baby won't you?"

"Alfredo, you're scaring me. I can't imagine a world without you and… What could I do for your wife anyway? I only know how to plough fields and look after the animals!"

"That's not true. You might not have finished school, but you're intelligent and when that fails, trust your instincts."

"What do you mean?"

"If Arianna needs something, your heart will point you in

the direction, Antonio. I know."

Why did he feel the need to say these things? Suddenly I remembered that only an hour ago I desired her physically, and that had never happened with a woman before. All the others seemed like a gaggle of geese in comparison, all the others weren't very nice to me, while Arianna….

Maybe I had been in love with her from the moment I first met her, but I didn't know it then. And Alfredo, who is the genius in the family, had understood all of this before I did. Why did he want to talk about it now? I would have preferred to have remained unaware of this terrible paradox: I adore my brother and I want his wife!…. As soon as his words touched my soul, I saw what was really inside me, and I turned towards the window and burst into tears.

Alfredo was shocked. "Antonio, what's the matter? What happened?"

But I cried in silence and refused to look him in the face. Then he understood.

"No, brother of mine," he said. "I'm not accusing you of anything. Calm down."

"I would never betray you!" I sobbed. " I'd rather die!"

"I know. Don't be so hard on yourself. Falling in love with Arianna is inevitable from the moment you meet her. If I were jealous husband, I would go and punch all of her colleagues who fight over who's going to give her a lift home after work. But I don't care because I know I'm the only one she loves. If I were to die, one day she would agree to be courted by someone else! But not now."

"No!" I replied angrily. "A woman could never love another man after having loved you!"

I know I shouldn't have said anything but I don't care because Alfredo got up and came over to hug me. When was the last time he hugged me? When?

I could have stayed where I was forever, I could have screamed "no woman will ever come between us!" But I'd already said enough. All I could do was hug him, cry, and keep silent.

When I felt him move way from me, I begged: "Don't get yourself killed Alfredo. Promise me that you won't get yourself killed."

But he didn't promise anything. He turned towards me and smiled sadly, saying: "Antonio, please. Go to bed now. I haven't finished working and it's really late."

Sleep! As if it were possible! But I did what he wanted and left him alone.

And so here I am in my room, writing this useless diary in attempt to stop my insomnia driving me crazy. Alfredo will finish his notes and will go back to Arianna who's waiting for him....

Once it was me who stayed awake and waited for him to come to bed. It was nineteen sixty five, the year Alfredo stayed up late to watch Perry Mason on TV. I wasn't interested in the television so I waited... But was it really nineteen sixty five?

He and Arianna will make love, but will they talk about the trial? Or will they remain in silence, thinking that tonight could be their last night together?

A nightmare. God, please let it be just a nightmare.

November 6th

Why hasn't Alfredo come home yet? It's four o'clock in the afternoon.

The trial should have started at nine o'clock in the morning, and he warned us that it could go on a while, he said that we should have lunch without him. My stomach's knotted.

Papa and Mama are having an afternoon nap. Of course they don't know that Alfredo was threatened. Only Arianna and I know.

She's sitting near the window in the living room, waiting, and every now and then we exchange glances but neither of us dare to admit that we are scared. At around half past three, I broke the silence. "Arianna….couldn't we phone the courthouse?"

"It's useless. The clerk will answer."

"But he'll know something. Even judges eat, when they're tired they take a break. We'll be able to find out they've called for a break."

Eventually she gave in and locked herself in the study to make the call. When she came out, she seemed happier.

"The trial has just finished. Alfredo's won, Collura has been acquitted."

"The acquittal of that thug doesn't make me feel any better. Where's my brother?"

"It's a long way from the courthouse in Palermo to the farm," my sister-in-law said encouragingly. "We'll have to wait."

How can she be so calm? She came and sat back down in front of the window, and I sat next to her, my elbow touching hers, to feel her warmth.

I need to be comforted, cuddled, but I'm not a child anymore and I have to fight the urge to hide my face in Arianna's lap. What would she think of me?

I'll lose her. Alfredo will save enough money to buy a house and then they'll leave this place...

I was mad to admit that I loved Arianna! My brother will do everything he can to take her away from here as soon as possible. Mad! What will I do without them? Will I only get to see them at Christmas and at Easter? It'll kill me.

Alfredo will spend his time spying on me to see if I make a move on his wife. Why did I tell him? Now I've lost both of them. Just the thought of not seeing them makes me ill; I want to vomit.

Nothing can fix the mess I've made. Unless Alfredo never comes home, and then Arianna will see me and this house as a kind of refuge and I'll get to look after her child.

Yes. Alfredo himself asked me. If he were to die, Arianna and Fabio would be mine.

Oh my God, what was I thinking! Maybe, for a moment, for less than a moment, I wished my brother were dead.

I must be mad. For a woman, for a damned female, what was I thinking!?! My Alfredo, why aren't you here?

God, forgive me. Let him come back immediately. Without anything happening to him, otherwise it would be like I killed him myself with my thoughts. God, free me from these terrible ideas. It's half past four. Why isn't he back?

Lord, if you want to punish me for my terrible thoughts, make it so that Arianna never looks me in the face again. It's what I deserve.

November 7th

It's over. The telephone call arrived yesterday, a quarter of an hour after I stopped writing this diary.

I can't believe that it was a robbery, as they said. A lawyer wins a case, leaves the courthouse, without the guards that he had been promised, gets into his car, and halfway home is stopped by three men in balaclavas. They smash the windows, pull my brother out of the car, rip off his watch, take his wallet, and before driving off in his car, shoot him! They shot him after they had taken everything? They weren't robbers. They were paid by the Messina family, but only Arianna and I know, and the authorities too, but they haven't got any hard proof.

My brother is lying in an open coffin. His noble face, serene: the face of a winner.

The funeral is tomorrow, and today we should have been celebrating Fabio's birthday!Why can't I cry? There's an emptiness inside me. It's as if a storm has swept my heart away.

November 9th

The silence inside the house is suffocating me. My mother is locked in one room, my father in another. Arianna is in the study and I don't know what the hell she's doing. Nobody wants to share their pain with the others. Alfredo was right: to my parents, Arianna will always be an outsider.

I want to talk to her, tell her that my brother made me promise…but it's not the right time. I've got no right to disturb her if she wants to cry alone. But if no one talks to me, I'll go mad.

I would scream like a madman if only to shatter this silence, but still the tears won't come. It's strange: if I could cry, I would feel better, and I've done everything I can think of to make myself cry. I've looked at all the things that remind me of Alfredo, his photos, his poems, even his bamboo cage that he built when he was fifteen. But it's useless: my eyes are dry.

My Arianna. If only I could cry in your arms! Where are you?

There I go again. I called her mine. I'm a monster.

Why do I have to torment myself? It's not my fault that Alfredo is dead and that now she is free. I didn't want Alfredo to die.

I couldn't have loved him more than I did. God saw fit to do what he did.

November 10th

I've finally talked to her. I found her in Alfredo's office behind piles of paper and the door was open, a sign that I could enter. I thought she was going through Alfredo's papers to find a clue that would help us incriminate the assassins. This is what I was thinking when I went up to her. She was writing something on a piece of paper. "What are you doing?" I asked.

"I'm filling out a transfer application."

The first thing I felt was disgust that her husband wasn't uppermost in her mind. I started with: "How can you think so clearly only two days after..." Then her words sank in.

"Transfer? What transfer?"

"From my office in Palermo, to one in Bologna. I know that my haste might seem strange to you, but if I don't apply in November, no one's going to be looking at anything in December because they'll all be thinking about Christmas, and I'll risk staying here for goodness knows how long."

I couldn't believe my ears. "Do you want to go back to Bologna?"

"My parents are there. You know full well that I only came to the South because I loved your brother."

"But your home is here now!"

"No, Antonio, I'm sorry. Your parents aren't mine. Life's different in Bologna."

That's true. And I can't tell her that I love her; she would look at me with horror. I've got to come up with other excuses to keep her here.

"But there's still loads to do!" I said. "We've got to find out who killed Alfredo!"

"Do you really think that'll happen in two or three months? The slowness of the Italian legal system is legendary. One day I'll be called to give evidence on the threats received by my husband, and I'll come back, I will, but years could go by before I hear anything."

"You can't leave!" I was reduced to begging. "I know that my parents weren't very affectionate at the beginning but now everything's different. They've lost a son and they've got a grandson. They adore Fabio. And I adore him too."

"Believe me, I've thought about that. But I've got to go. Everything here reminds me of Alfredo. Every object I see reminds me of him, I'd go mad if I were to stay. I'm too young to lock myself away on a farm with a black handkerchief on my head, I've got to start my life over somewhere else. Don't you understand, I'm not even twenty-six yet."

She wants to forget Alfredo. How can she forget him!

I could feel tears welling up in my eyes. Why now and not before, in front of my brother's body that was riddled with bullets? Is it true that she's all I care about? Is it true that I love her more than Alfredo and in these two days my emotions were on hold, waiting to see what Arianna would do? Maybe I hoped. What did I hope? Oh God, what if it were true that the dead watch us from up there! Brother of mine, will you ever be able to forgive me?

I tried to hide my tears from Arianna, but it was useless.

"Antonio, please don't. You won't lose your nephew. You can come to Bologna whenever you want."

Of course, Fabio's a good excuse for my tears. "I swore to my brother that I would take care of you and your children," I sobbed. "I swore because I thought that someone would try to kill him. But now you're trying to make me break my promise, because you're leaving!"

"Calm down. I'm quite capable of looking after myself, I've got a job, a house in Bologna, I've got everything. I know that a husband in love wants to entrust his family to someone, but I'm not helpless."

"I've lost my brother!" I shouted. "And now I've got to stay in a house with two old people that have nothing to say to one another!"

Then I covered my face with my hands, overcome with

emotion.

"I'm really sorry," she said. "I mean it. But remember, you're only twenty-one years old, and there are many changes in your life to come. One day you will have a family of your own, and everything else won't seem as important."

I will never love another woman, I will never have a family. But I couldn't tell her how I felt, I will never tell her. Why hasn't she realised? Why can't she read it in my eyes?

I couldn't speak. This is my punishment because I wanted my brother's wife, because for one damn moment, I hoped he would die. This is my penance.

I tried to control myself and then I said: "You're right Arianna. Excuse me. Will you write to me?"

"Of course I will, and you'll write to me. Let me know how the investigations are going."

Yes, this is my penance. This is the price I'll be paying for the rest of my life.

December 29th

She got want she wanted. She'll start work in Bologna on January third. She decided to spend New Year's with her family and so she left this morning.

Arianna was waiting for her taxi with her luggage piled up on the floor when my mother suddenly appeared. I was next to my sister-in-law, ready to say goodbye to her, my heart breaking. She had just given me her address in Bologna, when Mama came out of her room and stood at the top of the stairs.

I hadn't seen her for days. Alfredo's death had upset us all so much that nobody ate punctually; Papa and I ate sandwiches in the fields and Mama...well, who worried about her? As far as I was concerned she was the last person we had to worry about. You would have thought that the death of her favourite would have made her lose her mind, but the person I saw on the stairs was a woman possessed, if her bloodshot eyes and uncombed hair were anything to go by. She looked at Arianna's luggage and said: "So you're finally off then? I'll go and call the priest, get him to bless this house!"

My sister-in-law and I exchanged looks. We both knew that she wasn't the most affectionate mother-in-law, but we never thought she would go this far. Arianna, who was too polite to use the same tone, said:

"Mama, you're not well. Go back to bed, I wouldn't want you to fall down the stairs."

"You're right. It wouldn't surprise me if I did fall, seeing that the person who brought bad luck into this house is standing before me. We all know that Alfredo wouldn't be dead if you hadn't married him."

"Mama!" I shouted, "Stop it! You're delirious."

"No I'm not. It's the truth. She was the only one who knew that Alfredo had been threatened, and she did nothing to stop him going out there and getting himself killed!" She turned towards her daughter-in-law, with her eyes full of hate, and continued: "You were tired of living in the countryside, weren't you? You regretted marrying a Sicilian. You wanted him to die. You wanted to leave!"

I felt the blood surge to my head and I screamed: "Mama, I won't let you talk to her like that! Either you shut up, or I'll call a doctor and have you committed to a mental hospital!"

But sweet Arianna touched me on the shoulder, murmuring: "Be patient with your mother. Can't you see her heartbreak is driving her insane?"

She was interrupted by the sound of a car horn: the taxi had arrived. I got Arianna's two suitcases and threw myself out of the door, dodging the insults that my mother was hurling at Arianna.

I don't know why I didn't offer to accompany Arianna in my own car. Maybe, subconsciously, I didn't want to help her abandon me, or I was worried about crying at the station. I gave the two suitcases to the driver and paid him.

When I went back inside to get the rest of the suitcases, Arianna was putting Fabio's coat on and saying: 'take a good look at this child' or something like that. But I didn't want to hear anymore. I grabbed the last two suitcases and took them outside to the taxi.

Everything was ready at last. My sister-in-law was looking at me strangely from the doorstep, her cheeks burning red with rage. I took my nephew in my arms and gave him a farewell kiss, then I said goodbye to her. I swear that she was cold, that she even turned her head slightly so that my lips wouldn't touch the corner of her mouth. Oh Mama, what have you done?

"Bye." I said, trying to stay calm. "I'll write to you."

"Okay," she replied, and she climbed into the taxi without saying anything else. She didn't even smile.

What had that wicked mother-in-law said to her? What could she have said that was worse than what I'd already heard?

On the way up to my room, I passed my mother on the landing and had to fight the urge to throw her down the stairs.

And now it's all over. I've lost all the people that I loved, and I'm here alone with a father who doesn't say much and a mother to whom I never want to speak to again.

I can't describe what I'm feeling but if I manage to survive all of this, it must mean that I'm immortal.

March 21st, 1972

Papa. Only he could tell me what to do. He's always loved me, always understood because we are so alike, even though he hasn't got much time for me. He has given me some advice, it might turn out to be the good advice, but it certainly wasn't what I wanted to hear.

I was wandering round the farm for half an hour before I found him: he was supervising the pruning of the vines. "Papa," I ventured, "can I have a word?"

"Go ahead." But there were two farmhands just in front of us, and I had to make him understand that I wanted to speak to him alone.

"Please Papa. It's important."

He must have understood from the tone of my voice that it wasn't about the usual ill animal or a cow that wasn't doing her duty. He took me by the arm and led me away from the workers.

"It's about Arianna," I said. "She's been gone for three months and she hasn't replied to any of my letters. We don't know how she's getting on, or how the baby is. He is our only heir after all."

"So what? What do you want to do about it?"

"I thought, if you could do without me for a couple of days, I could go up north to see if my sister-in-law and my nephew are okay."

"Right. And if you were to find a job in Bologna, would you stay there?"

I was speechless. "What makes you think that I would stay?"

"Because I know the ridiculous things men do for women."

I could feel my face burning. "How did you figure that out?"

"I'm a man too. I've got eyes. I saw how you looked at her across the table. And if she didn't understand, then she really is stupid."

"No she isn't stupid. She was far too much in love with Alfredo to notice me. And I never told her! I would never tell anyone!"

"I know you wouldn't."

He wasn't rebuking me, he was supporting me, man to man. I spoke to him from my heart: "Papa I'm a farmer. I would

58

never leave my farm. I swear I only want to know if Arianna and Fabio are okay."

"I believe you but you can forget it. She's a university graduate, she's not one of us. I'm sure she's got herself a new life up there, and that's why she doesn't reply to your letters. You, however, will find another woman who is right for you. One who loves the countryside as much as you do."

My disappointment must have been written all over my face.

"What the hell!" exclaimed Papa. "What did she have that was so special?"

"You'll never understand."

"Are you trying to tell me she was the most beautiful girl in the world? No more so than any of the others that you've always ignored. You loved her because she was Alfredo's, just like you would have loved his dog, if he had had one."

He's comparing Arianna to a dog! I would have been offended if I hadn't known that Papa always expresses himself crudely, and anyway I understood what he meant.

"Very well," I said curtly. "I won't go. It would be humiliating if I got all the way to Bologna only to discover that Arianna doesn't write to me, because she can't be bothered."

My father slapped me warmly on the back, saying: "I knew I could count on your good sense."

Was that all? Will my good sense help me sleep at night, after months and months of insomnia? Will my good sense help me forget that my mother has mortally offended Arianna and now Arianna wants to erase an entire period of her life? Or is it true that a college graduate would never stoop so low as to acknowledge an ignoramus like me as a relative?

I love my farm and I'm proud to be a farmer. But today, for the first time, I cursed my circumstances.

September 15th, 1972

I got the doctor to prescribe me pills to help me sleep. He says that I'm too young to be relying on sleeping pills and mustn't take more than the recommended minimum dose: not more than half a tablet at night. It isn't enough, with half a pill I only manage to sleep for two hours and two hours aren't very much if you have to do a full day's work. At the moment, I'm helping Papa with the vines and I'm very tired.

I thought about taking a whole pill, despite what the doctor said, but if I finish the box too soon and I ask him to prescribe me another, I doubt he won't notice. No pharmacist will give me the damn stuff without a prescription.

I've got to think this through properly. The instructions say that the effect of the medicine is strengthened by alcohol: great, I'll have a few tonight. Let's see what happens. If I die, it'll be better than living with insomnia.

January 3rd, 1973

My experiment worked: I take half a tablet at night after having drunk loads of wine at dinner and I manage to sleep. Or rather, I'm no longer overwhelmed by bad thoughts, and during the day, I work so hard that I haven't got time to think. My father was right: the land is my flesh and my blood; the land is the only thing that won't betray me.

Things would be even better if my mother had asked the doctor for sleeping pills too. She hasn't been the same since Alfredo's death; she's short with everyone, angry, unbearable. Yesterday the cleaner resigned in tears, but sadly Papa and I can't resign, we listen to Mama's screams and exchange glances, both of us thinking, *Poor old thing, she's not well.* If I'm being honest, it's my father who tells me to be kind to my mother. I think that she's got no right to behave like she does: she's not the only one who's lost Alfredo! She knows nothing about how I suffer. She knows nothing about my sleeping pills and my drunken nights. She knows nothing about the time I spend when I'm not at work in front of a photograph of my brother.

I got the nicest photograph of him framed, I put it in my room and I talk to it as if it were a living person. My parents would think I was crazy if they knew. But in that photo his eyes are smiling and they give me a sense of comfort, because only if I see Alfredo smiling, can I convince myself that he's forgiven me.

December 2nd, 1974

Now I'm really on my own. My father has died of a heart attack. He'd had high blood pressure for a while, and I wouldn't exclude the possibility that my mother's behaviour raised it even further. Poor Papa, the amount of insults he had to put up with!

Now I've got the weight of the farm on my shoulders. *Papa, what have you done? I still needed your help.*

Tomorrow, I'll write to Arianna to tell her that Papa is dead. It won't change anything, I know, but if I do get a frosty letter of condolence from her, at least I know that she reads my letters before she throws them away.

June 14th, 1975

I haven't got much time to write in this diary anymore I'm working so hard.

I used to enjoy writing a little before going to bed, but now in the evenings I'm so drunk that I can hardly make out the lines on the page.

The alcohol also helps me to escape the oppressive atmosphere in this house. Papa's not here anymore, Mama and

I have nothing to say to one another. The silence is deafening! At seven o'clock every evening, when the farmhands have finished work, we all go to bar to get drunk. I go home drunk, but all I get from my mother is a dirty look as I pass her in the kitchen on my way upstairs to my room. I drink some more before I take a pill. I don't know what will happen to me, and I don't particularly care.

Every now and then, in the mornings as soon as I get up, I read back through my diary and it hits me just how much time has slipped by. Three and half years since Alfredo died, and no one has been brought to justice for his killing. Why is justice so slow in arriving?

Arianna was right when she said 'years could pass.' But if no one does anything, I'll do something myself.

I must find time to see Randazzo the lawyer, who was Alfredo's colleague and business partner, and his best friend. I'll ask him why the investigations into this case have never got off the ground.

My mother was sixty years old yesterday. I didn't forget; I just didn't feel like spending any time with her. Actually, I had dinner out with friends. When I got home, she was waiting for me in the living room, ready for bed, in a night dress and dressing grown. And she did something she'd never done before. She asked me why I was so late.

"I had to talk to Pino," I replied, "about the rent for the stud bull."

"You talked about the bull until eleven o'clock at night?"

"Well naturally we went to the bar afterwards to celebrate the deal."

"How much have you drunk, Antonio? You do realise you're turning into an alcoholic, don't you?"

"Ahah. So you've noticed then? I didn't think you cared about what I was up to! And neither did I think that you cared about something so trivial as my health."

"You can't run a farm with an alcohol-addled brain."

Ahhh. So that's what this is all about. I replied: "I've been running the farm perfectly well. I've fired two farmhands who were useless, something that Papa would never have done because he was too good. Now shut up and let me go to bed, tomorrow there's the sowing to do."

I headed towards the stairs but she called me back in a tone of voice that was unusually sweet. "Antonio, did you know I turned sixty today?"

Maybe it was an attempt at reconciliation. Maybe turning sixty had made her reflect on past mistakes: she realised that she had alienated herself from her only remaining relative, the only one who could help her in her old age. But I ignored her olive branch, for I'm certain that it's her fault that Arianna has never replied to my letters, even though I not sure exactly why.

"I didn't forget your birthday," I replied. I've even brought you a present. Here..."

I pulled a packet out of my pocket and tossed it to her from the stairs: it was a box of sweets. I enjoyed the face she made as she turned it over in her hands.

"Candy?" she said, shocked.

"Right. To make your mouth sweeter, seeing that your words are always bitter."

It seemed like a good joke, but I'm not as good as Alfredo. He would have thought of something funnier.

I've just discovered something terrible: the investigations into the murder of my brother are about to be "archived," filed away without charges being brought. The lawyer, Randazzo, who was very sorry, said that officially Alfredo's death was caused by a robbery and that there was no evidence against that family of *Mafiosi* against which he had fought so hard. Well there's a surprise! Al Capone went to jail for tax evasion even though not a single judge had uncovered evidence to support the accusations!

They all know that Alfredo was threatened but obviously every single member of the Messina family had an alibi for that evening. And there are always kids willing to take Mafia money to stage a fake robbery that ends in death. You can't check every single alibi of the street kids in Sicily.

But why did they promise Alfredo a police escort and then not give it to him? Was the judge also paid by the Mafia? Who's ever going to stir up that hornets nest? Randazzo's accepted the judgement, but I'll never give up! The only thing my brother wanted to do was to throw the Messina clan in jail, and if they get away with it, he gave his life for nothing!

It can't end like this. Alfredo had a wife who has a law degree. She'll know what to do.

I'll write to her again. Whatever the reason for Arianna's silence, she wouldn't be indifferent to the idea that Alfredo's death will never be vindicated. She's got to come to Palermo, contact the right people, she can't stay in Bologna and do nothing while Alfredo's memory is being dishonoured.

Yes, I'll write to her. I can't believe that her damned pride that keeps her away from us is stronger than the love that bound her to her husband. She will come. She will come, bringing a flicker of light into my life.

She hasn't replied. My last letter has met the same fate as all the others.

Anyway, that woman was overrated. She wasn't worthy of Alfredo. She's not fighting to avenge his death; I can never forgive her.

My father was right, as always: I loved her because she was part of Alfredo, but if this is an example of how she behaves now, she is no longer the woman I once loved.

What will she be doing in Bologna? Has she got another man? Shouldn't she be teaching Fabio to honour the memory of his father, who died a hero?

Oh God, why can't I just drop everything and go up there and see what's happened to my brother's family? Who's stopping me? My father is dead and I don't give a shit what Mama thinks. But something stops me every time I get it into my head to go to Bologna.

Maybe it's the fear of finding Arianna indifferent, or worse hostile, the fear of finding something that will deepen my pain instead of erasing it. I want to remember the sweet expression on her face when she said 'be patient with your mother.' I couldn't bear to destroy that image.

I won't chase after Arianna, and the next time that I find the courage to write to her, it'll be to reproach her for her silence and to say farewell. But not yet, I haven't got the strength.

Now however I've got to find away to avenge Alfredo's death. But who can help me? My brother's absence tortures me on days like today, when a sudden downpour interrupts my work and forces me to stay in my room doing nothing. So I open this diary and reread some of the pages and my pain becomes physical, as if I were missing a part of my body. Alfredo, why don't you help me? Why don't you come to me with evidence that could incriminate your murderer? I'm not afraid of your ghost.

I keep a candle lit in front of his photos, and while I'm talking to him, I always expect him to show his presence by making the flame sway to the left or to the right. I ask him questions to which he only has to reply yes or no to: flame to the right for a yes, flame to the left for a no. At times, I really do believe that he is giving me the correct answer and I'm comforted as if he were here. And I'm also certain that a couple of times my mother has heard me from the other side of the door, and that she thinks I'm crazy. But I don't care.

September 24th, 1980

I've written to Arianna, and this time it really is the last time. This is my farewell:

"My darling Arianna,

Now I can use that word: darling. I swore that I would never tell you how much I loved you, out of loyalty to the memory of my brother, but now I can be honest with you because you will never receive another letter from me.

I even physically desired you that evening when you were waiting for him to return, and he didn't come back. I'm a monster. If only you would write and tell me that I'm not a monster: it would at least break the silence. But I know that you would never deign to do so. You don't care about Alfredo, and you don't care about me, I only hope that you're bringing up my nephew well.

I'm thirty now. I've been so consumed by my love for you that I've never even looked at another woman. I know that I can't continue like this. My mother wants me to marry because our land needs an heir: okay then, maybe I will get married. But

I want you to know that if one day I decide a get a wife, it'll only be because I love this land. I'll find a dull woman, someone for whom I have no feelings, because the love that I had for you messed up my life, and I don't want to feel anything anymore. I just want to be left in peace.

I'll even let my mother choose my bride: what does it matter; it's not you.

Farewell forever,
Antonio"

October 10th, 1984

My mother was operated on last week: she had a tumour in her uterus so they took everything out. At the moment she's got to stay in bed to stop any blood loss, but there's nothing wrong with her appetite, she looks fine to me. The only thing she complains about is the absence of a daughter-in-law to help her. It's a dig at my single status. She only thinks about herself. But I've got the vines to think about.

November 11th, 1985

Today my mother got food poisoning and you would have thought she was about to die by the way she behaved — she sent the housekeeper rushing out to the fields to find me. I thought she wanted a doctor, but no, all she wanted to do was to nag me about getting married.

"You're thirty-five years old," she said for the umpteenth time. "When are you going to get yourself a girlfriend?"

"Mama, you didn't drag me away from work just to ask me about a girlfriend, did you?"

"You don't understand. I'm not well, and before I die I want to meet your son."

Does she think the cancer's advancing? I hadn't dared ask.

"I know and I promised you that I would, sooner or later."

"No, not 'sooner or later.' I want to get to know my daughter-in-law now, I want to be sure that she's a good woman."

"What do you care? As long as she gives me children, what does it matter if she's a bitch who makes me unhappy?"

My words hit home: her eyes were filled with sorrow.

"Do you really believe that I never loved you just because your brother's death left me in pieces?"

"No. Maybe you would have preferred to have lost me, but that's understandable: I would have preferred to die in his place too."

"Don't say that, my son. You were both born of my womb and I loved you both. If you felt that I favoured Alfredo, it was because of something that happened before you were born. You see, your father wasn't my first lover."

For one terrible moment I thought she was about to tell me something that I would never have accepted: that Alfredo was somebody else's son. Lord, I could have killed her.

"Mama, what do you mean?"

"When I was twenty years old, I was in love with a university student, Renato. He was like your brother: more intelligent than average, studious. But my parents didn't let me marry him because he was poor, and I was poor too: together, we would have starved. In protest, I refused to be courted for years, and then along came your father. I confess I didn't love him when I married him; I married him because he was rich. But then I grew to care about him because he was a wonderful person, and I never regretted choosing him. I had two sons with him and Alfredo, strangely, reminded me of Renato. They had the same brilliant intelligence, the same desire to change the world. It was as if God had wanted to give me back my first love. I had to worship him; I didn't have a choice. You were more like your father, but that doesn't mean that you meant nothing to me! I tried to treat both my sons equally, and if at times I failed, please forgive me."

That's how I got answers to questions that had remained unanswered for years, but now it's all clear, I don't care. I can't imagine my mother young and in love with a certain Renato who was similar to Alfredo! What does it matter now anyway?

"That's nothing," I said. "That's not why I have to forgive you. I wasn't envious of Alfredo, I worshipped him too. That's not how you hurt me. It's something else entirely."

"What else have I done to you? I swear I have no idea!"

"You really don't know? Arianna? You were nasty to her, it was you who pushed her away from me! You must have said something to her, otherwise she would have replied to my letters. That's why I'll never be able to forgive you." At last, after years of silence, I had told her.

"Arianna? How could you still be in love with that woman after fourteen years?" She really did seem confused. "I really haven't understood you at all, have I? I thought you were obsessed with avenging the death of Alfredo. I thought that's why you drank. I can hear you, when you speak to his photo. Oh, I don't know what's going on anymore!"

You're right Mama. How can you fathom something that not even I understand? I don't know whether the darkness that's slowly killing me is Alfredo's absence or Arianna's absence, or the damned day when I betrayed them both with my shameful thoughts.

"I don't want to talk about it," I replied.

"Arianna. I didn't hate her, believe me. I was jealous, just as I would have been of any woman who took Alfredo away from me. His time, I mean. His free time, not his love, because Alfredo was incapable of loving anyone but himself."

"That's not true," I protested.

"It's true. But I forgave him anyway."

Poor Mama. We were enemies for so many years without realising that we were so similar and so close, united in our unrequited love. For him.

I would have liked to have been able to cry with her for what we have lost, but tears haven't fallen from my eyes for years, not since Arianna left.

I kissed my mother, trying not to be repulsed by her sweaty forehead and the smell of vomit on her night dress. She hadn't expected a kiss from me, and her face crumpled as if she was about to cry.

"Antonio..."

"No," I interrupted her," Let's not talk about the past anymore. Tell me about your plans for the mother of my children, I'm sure you've already chosen her. You have, haven't you?"

"I've got an idea, yes. Such a pretty girl, you're bound to like her. Can't you guess who it is?"

"No..."

"Eva Di Trapani."

"Tina's little sister? That tiny little blonde thing? No way."

"Are you serious, Mama? She's only a child. I was sixteen when she was born."

"Yes, and now you're thirty five and she's nineteen, she's a woman now. She's so pretty that if you don't hurry up and ask for her hand, someone else will."

I don't want a beautiful girl, I'd rather avoid comparisons with Arianna. "I don't know what she looks like. I mean, I saw her at Tina's wedding, but she was only two years old."

"Do you want see her now? It'll be easy. Organise a party with those four friends you go drinking with: invite them and their women, Tina and her husband, and ask her to bring her sister because there's an extra male. The Di Trapani's will be so happy when they hear of your intentions towards her. Don't you realise you're the best catch in the neighbourhood? What father wouldn't want to give you their daughter."

"She's so young, Mama. Why does it have to be her?"

"It was my husband's dream to unite the two families for the bordering lands, his friendship with Nunzio. I owe it to him, to the memory of your father."

Yes, I remember when he talked about 'giving' me Tina. Maybe my mother is full of remorse too, after all. She knows she didn't love my poor father enough.

"Okay," I said, "let's have this party and I'll get to know Eva, but I can't promise you anything..."

"I only want you to promise me that you won't get drunk at the party. I know Giovanni Di Trapani, he would never try to betroth his daughter to an alcoholic."

Yes, I promised her. I love my farm enough to take a woman, even if it isn't Arianna, just to have an heir. I might neglect my wife but my mother will understand. She knows that the fate of every countrywoman is to remain at home alone while her husband is out in the fields: it was her fate too.

She probably likes Eva because she was like her; considered by her parents to be quality goods to be sold to a rich farmer, and thank goodness my father was an excellent husband. I won't be as good as him. I might love my child, but I won't be able to be anything more than be polite to my wife.

If Arianna hadn't taken Fabio away, I would be teaching him how to manage the farm by now, he would have been my heir. I wouldn't have to get married.

Fabio must be fifteen now. I wonder if he looks like Alfredo?

I feel strangely uneasy when I think of him. I've got to forget about my nephew.

71

The party went really well. At the beginning I was panicking, but everything changed when Tina arrived. I hadn't seen her for years! My old playmate has put on weight; she certainly wouldn't be able to go riding anymore. As soon as I saw her, I hugged her, thinking: look at her, the woman who could have married Alfredo, changing the course of my life! She's fatter with the odd grey hair but still smells of hay. What I wouldn't give to relive those days once more!

"Antonio," she hissed, "don't squeeze me so tightly, my husband's here."

I reluctantly detached myself from her, and suddenly I realised that if she did have a younger sister, who looked like her, I would want her. She could take me back to happier times.

I was staring at Tina, thinking how quickly time had taken its pitiless toll on her body, when she said: "This is my little sister Eva."

At first I only noticed her dazzling smile which chilled me to the bone. It was the type of smile that women saved for Alfredo, not for me. No woman should be allowed to smile like that now he is dead.

"Good evening," she said in a lilting voice. I looked at her and she really was beautiful: blonde, pale skinned and curvy, with two green almond shaped eyes. Alfredo would have liked her; she looked just like the woman in the posters that he plastered the walls of our room with when we were kids. I can't remember her name, but she looked like Eva.

I must admit that my mother has made an excellent choice: this little blonde reminds me of the past so much, she breaks my heart.

I danced with her all night, but we didn't say much to each other. All we did was dance and look at each other in the eyes.

Poor little thing, she's only nineteen, and after she left school at thirteen, her parents kept her locked away to stop her falling in love with a poor bastard: what does she know about men? Nothing!

Maybe that's also why my mother chose her. A naïve girl won't know the difference between a lump like me and some other suitor. She'll accept me.

I felt uneasy then, as if the wedding was already a done deal. I stopped dancing, surrendering Eva to another partner, and went to pour myself a drop of wine. I prefer spirits to wine, have done for a while now: the same effect for less liquid intake. I know my mother told me not to drink during the party but then I said to myself: well everyone's drinking here, why should I be the only one sober.

A little while later, Tina came to sit down next to me. She was breathing heavily; fat women shouldn't dance. "Hello old friend," she said. "Are you feeling your age?"

"I want to marry your sister," I blurted out. I was scared I wouldn't have the courage to say anything had I waited any longer.

"Are you drunk?" asked Tina, laughing.

"I might be, but I'm serious. She not engaged to anyone, is she?"

"No, she's too young."

"But you were her age when you got married."

She stared at me trying to understand how serious I was. "If you're not joking, I could ask my parents."

"Good, but first ask the lady in question, and tell her that I'm in a hurry."

"Why are you in a hurry? You'd need to get to know one another first!"

"I haven't got time to wait," I whispered mysteriously. I really couldn't wait, I was afraid I would change my mind.

"Antonio, what's got into you?"

"It's just I've got to get married immediately because I'm expecting a baby."

Tina burst out laughing and clapped me on the back. "Good one! I almost fell for it!"

It wasn't a particularly good one. Alfredo would never have made a joke like that. It was banal.

Anyway, I'll marry the mirror image of my brother's ideal woman. Of course I will.

Here closes a chapter of my life and another one is about to start that doesn't merit being recorded in a diary. I will never write anything again. I've been drinking too much for a while now, and I think my writing is suffering. My hands shake so much that the letters are almost illegible.

Then again, what have I got left to write about? Alfredo's death hasn't been avenged, his wife has forgotten about him, and there's nothing left in my heart but desperation and hate.

Part 2

Eva's Diary (1985-1990)

November 14th, 1985

Today Tina told me that there's going to be a huge party at our neighbour's house, the Altavillas, and that we're all invited. Their friendship with my family goes back to when my parents were very young, but it's a long time since I've seen any of them. Years ago there was talk of marriage between Tina and one of the Altavillas who died when I was a child. Luckily, my sister always knew that this Alfredo wasn't interested in her, so while he was away studying in Bologna, Tina married someone else. Thank goodness she did: he came back from Bologna with a wife and Tina would have been cast aside after having waited for so long for nothing!

So why now? Tina says that Alfredo's brother has his eye on me. But I've never even met him! I will chose a husband myself and only when I'm good and ready. Arranged marriages belong to medieval times.

Tina says: 'Give him a chance, run your eye over this Antonio, he's got beautiful eyes and a good heart.' Tina grew up with him, so she knows what she's talking about. But a thirty-five year old man is practically a pensioner compared to me. And anyway, if he is such a good catch like she says he is, why didn't he get married ten years ago?

We'll have to wait and see. Nobody knows if he actually does like me, and anyway I'll be the one to decide; my parents will never force me to marry a man I don't like. I'll go to the party, it'll be an excuse to get out of the house, and I'll be able to put an evening dress on and show myself off a bit. This Antonio won't be the only one there. There will be others...

It was a lovely party. I met the mysterious Antonio, he's quite a handsome man, but he hardly said anything all evening so I don't know what he's like character wise. I did however get the impression that he likes his drink.

But the amazing thing is, even though he didn't pay me a single compliment all evening, he's already told Tina that he wants to marry me! I don't understand why he's in such a hurry. I haven't got much of a dowry so I already knew I would be chosen for my looks not my money, but I thought he could have at least said something along the lines of 'you're pretty.' I wouldn't want to find myself with a husband who doesn't know how to please a woman.

All Tina talks about are the advantages of this marriage. Apart from the fact that my children and I will be the heirs to a huge farm, my sister's convinced that an older man will be able to make me happier than a younger one could. It's because a younger man starts off married life by saying things like "don't do this" and "you should be like this", to try and shape his wife into what they see as the ideal woman. An older man however doesn't behave like that: he considers a younger wife to be a gift from heaven and so is eternally grateful for her presence. He indulges her every whim and puts her on a pedestal; he wouldn't dare upset her in case she left him.

I don't think men spend that much time thinking about that sort of thing to be honest, and anyway I don't believe that Antonio is the type to stick his wife on a pedestal. However, I could accept the engagement as a trial, so that I can get to know this mysterious Antonio better. An engagement can always be broken off, and if I realise that things aren't working out, then I'll be off too.

Today my engagement was officially announced, but you could say that I've spent more time in the company of my future mother-in-law than my future husband. While Antonio chatted to my parents, donna Elena Altavilla, obviously wanting to spend some time alone with me, offered to show me around the house where I'll be living when I am married. The house is enormous. Actually, while we were wandering around the rooms, she let me in on some distressing secrets which have given me pause for thought.

Donna Elena is seventy years old but she's still a handsome woman. If you saw her, you would think she was in perfect health, but she told me that she's suffering from an awful illness and wants to see Antonio married before she dies. She even asked me why I had agreed to the engagement and I told her the truth: to me, it was just a trial run and if there were roses between us, they would bloom.

I think she was satisfied with my response. I really do think however, that if I had said I only wanted Antonio for his money, she would have shown more enthusiasm! Seeing that I was being honest, she began to confide in me too. To begin with, she's already been operated on once for cancer, but what her son doesn't know is that she is convinced that she has secondary tumours in her intestines: she hasn't seen a doctor but she's losing blood. - Antonio mustn't know for now. - she said.

I don't know why a mother should want to hide something like that from her son, but after listening to what else she had to tell me, I've come to the conclusion that their relationship is rather strange.

She begged me to be patient with Antonio, as no one, not even she, has ever loved him enough. "My son," she said, "has always underestimated himself. He thought he was ugly just because he didn't have the seductive beauty of his brother Alfredo. He thought he was stupid just because he wasn't a genius like Alfredo. He lived in his brother's shadow, and withdrew when he died, but I can assure you that he is anything but stupid. He's a sensitive boy, but he hides it well. He used to keep a diary when he was younger, and once I found it and read a couple of pages. I know I shouldn't have, but you know what mothers are like. That morning Antonio had made his own bed but he'd done it badly, so I went into his room to redo it, and I saw his diary on the table. I read enough to understand that my son writes incredibly well, he writes like a poet. He was only fifteen at the time and all he talked about was Alfredo. His idol. Antonio has suffered greatly, and if you ever learn how to tame him, you'll be the master of his heart."

At this point, I had to ask: "But he's thirty five years old, don't you think it's strange that he has never loved another woman. Has he ever been hurt?"

Donna Elena looked at me for a moment, as though she was considering telling me the truth, then she led me into a strange room. It's where Antonio sleeps: she hadn't shown it to me because when we are married, we'll have a different, bigger room.

"Look," she said, "this is where Antonio and his brother slept when they were boys, and now Antonio sleeps here alone, although you would think that Alfredo had never left. Do you see anything strange?"

I looked around the room. There were strange objects hung on the wall, including a kind of cage made from stars, and an old gun, and one wall was completely occupied by a kind of altar. Placed on the top, was a photograph of an extremely handsome man that I vaguely remembered meeting when I was little, and then I realised that it was Alfredo. There was a

78

lit candle in front of the photo. "Oh Christ!" I cried. "Where does he think he is? In church?"

"Antonio would be very angry if he knew that I had shown you this room. It's his sanctuary. Everything you see belonged to Alfredo. This evening I'm showing you things that I shouldn't really show you, but I trust you. Antonio worshipped his brother's memory. Has anyone ever told you how he died?"

"He was killed by the Mafia, wasn't he?"

"Yes he was, but they made it look like a burglary, and they never found any evidence against the killers. That's one of Antonio's obsessions, but there's another." I saw Donna Elena hesitate, but finally she continued, "He had a silly infatuation with Alfredo's wife, and obviously he's not able to forgive himself. He never declared his love for her. That's why he's never had a girlfriend."

Now I understand. I remember seeing Alfredo's wife years ago — a good-looking woman. But what I remember much more clearly is that she went back to Bologna far too hastily after Alfredo's death, and people talked. People always do, usually about things that don't concern them in the slightest.

"Listen, continued the woman, "the day Arianna left, I made a terrible mistake. I accused her of messing around with Antonio's feelings. I didn't know at the time that she had given him her address so that he could write to her. I treated her as if she were a silly airhead who was enjoying herself by seducing a naïve boy. I swear to God, I said those things because I really did believe that they were true, but while I was speaking, I noticed the surprise with which she was staring at me. She knew nothing of Antonio's feelings. For Christ's sake, she was the only one in the house who hadn't noticed. I was the one who, stupidly, told her. It was too late by then to take it back: my daughter-in-law was mortally offended. She showed me her son and said, 'Take a good look at your grandson, because you'll never see him again,' and she's kept her promise. She's never once been in touch. She's never replied to Antonio's letters, and he suspects that it's my fault, even though he doesn't know exactly how. I feel guilty for what I've done to my bachelor son. I've tried to right this wrong I've done him, by finding him a good girl who's right for him, and really do hope that it's you. Your beauty could make him forget Arianna."

I felt sorry for donna Elena, and for Antonio too. After all those revelations, I can't think of him as a mature man anymore. In my eyes he's no longer a thirty-five year old man, but an innocent boy who has been wounded by the betrayal of the woman he loved. It would be good if I could make him forget his one young love! I'm almost excited by the challenge. Certainly, winning the heart of a man so damaged won't be easy.

But I am the most beautiful girl here and anyway, I like challenges.

June 14th, 1986

I'm getting married tomorrow. I wonder if anyone else has gone along with an engagement just because they're too lazy to put a stop to it. But the big day's arrived, and it's too late to change my mind. I can't complain about Antonio's behaviour over these past six months. He's been very kind, and Tina was right when she said that he would never dare to order me around. But he hasn't awoken any passion in me yet.

Maybe I hoped that he would have confided in me, that he would have shown me his vulnerable side. What was I hoping for? That one day he would have burst into tears while telling me about his brother and his sister-in-law, and he would have let me console him? Yes, something along those lines would have awoken something inside me, but he never talks about himself, let alone about his past. I think he goes out of his way not to talk about the people who were dear to him. But I do think that the less he mentions them, the more he thinks about them. His eyes are sad.

Neither can I shake off the feeling that he drinks too much, although he has never been drunk in my presence. At times he does seem a little dazed, and he goes to the bathroom far too often for someone who is only thirty-six years old. I doubt he has prostate problems at his age! There are still loads of things I don't know about him, things which I'll only discover after the wedding. Maybe I crazy for marrying him: who marries someone for curiosity's sake?

I can sense the fragility that he hides, and I know that I could love him if he were to open his heart to me. I've got to use the art of seduction. After all none of the other suitors I've had were any better than Antonio. None of them were handsome, none of them were rich, and most of them were coarse and vulgar and would have behaved as if they were my 'masters.'

No, I mustn't regret my decision.

I've just spent my first night as a married woman and I should be overjoyed, but actually I could cry with rage.

It's not that Antonio was violent; on the contrary, he spent the whole time of asking me whether he was hurting me. And I replied: "no you're not hurting me, keep going." My married sisters have always told me that a loving husband behaves in a certain way: kisses on the mouth, on the breasts, but he did nothing like that. My sisters will ask me if I have had an orgasm and I don't even know what one is yet.

I'm sure he had an orgasm because after yelling for a short time, he relaxed and rolled off me. I was waiting for some tenderness, but do you know what he said? He asked me when my last period was!

"What do you want to know that for?" I replied, and he said, "I want to know if you're fertile." Is this why he married me? Just to have children?

I'm outraged. Doubly outraged, because when he got out of bed, he said: "I've got to go, it's the last day of the harvest." No cuddles for me then, just chores. Get the wife pregnant and oversee the harvesting. Both chores.

As if it couldn't get any worse, I saw a box of sleeping tablets on his bedside table. That's why he slept so deeply after taking my virginity, while I lay there, shaking with the pain. His first night with me, as a married man, and he takes sleeping pills.

After he had got dressed, he looked at me happily and said: "If I get back late, don't worry. We're expected to go out this evening to celebrate the end of the harvest. They'll all be congratulating me on my marriage and I'll sure I'll have one too many. You'll forgive me if I'm a little merry when I get back this evening, won't you?"

I already knew that he drank, and anyway there are other things that I need to forgive him for.

June 17th

Last night they brought him home so drunk that his friends had to carry him up the stairs: I couldn't have managed on my own. Then I undressed him, put him to bed and gave him a coffee saying: "Drink this, it'll sober you up a bit."

He seemed mortified. "I'm sorry, I don't usually drink this much, but my friends made me -"

"Go and find someone else to make a fool of," I replied, irritated, and I was about to continue when his voice took on a beseeching note: "You're such a sweet bride. You deserve a better husband than me."

At that point my anger melted away. I remembered the advice of my mother-in-law: If Antonio is convinced that he is good for nothing, then his wife's task is to make him believe in himself. How though? But while I was asking myself what I could do for him, he said something awful:

"Take that dress off. It's got blood on it."

There was nothing on the dress, but he seemed so convinced that I had to check. "What? Blood? Where?"

"There's a stain there. Can't you see it?" he repeated.

"Antonio you've drunk so much that it wouldn't surprise me if you saw a hippo on my dress."

He didn't say anything more but turned and started looking for something on his bedside table.

"Antonio! You're not thinking of taking a sleeping pill are you?"

"And how am I supposed to sleep without a sleeping pill?"

Poor me. Things are worse than I thought. I don't want to have children with a drunk. Tomorrow I'll go and get some birth control pills.

July 13th

Donna Elena is dead. I'm very sorry, she was very affectionate towards me, but Antonio seems indifferent. Maybe what she said was true then, that he never forgave his mother.

The family doctor came to sign the death certificate, and while the place was full of relatives and friends who had come to pay their respects, I took the opportunity to take the doctor aside for a few moments. There were some important matters I had to discuss with him: the first thing I asked was whether he had ever noticed that my husband was a drunk.

"No, I haven't," he admitted. "But I haven't always been the Altavillas' doctor. Your husband came to me a couple of years ago having left his previous doctor because he hadn't wanted to prescribe him any more sleeping pills. Actually my colleague was wrong to refuse. Antonio is hooked on benzodiazepines and he would suffer withdrawal symptoms if they were to be withheld from him."

That too!

"He drinks too much," I insisted, "and he's starting to see strange things. Stains that don't exist, spiders on the walls..."

"Really? I'll keep an eye on him then."

"Doctor, l don't want to have children with a drunk. I'm taking birth control pills, but my husband doesn't know, and there would be trouble if he were to find out. He only married me because he wanted an heir."

Now I had the doctor's full attention. He stared at me as if he were thinking: such a beautiful woman, and that's why he married her?

"What would happen," I asked, "if my husband was worried about my fertility and sent me to a gynaecologist? He would find out!"

"What could I do? I can't falsify the results."

"I know you can't. But you are Antonio's doctor. You could tell him that it's his fault that I'm not pregnant. It's his fault because he drinks too much. Could you do that?"

"Well, yes, I could. An alcoholic's sperm can weaken."

"Okay, if you could say something. It's for Antonio's good too. He really wants a son, so it could encourage him to stop drinking if you were to say something like that to him."

"Madam, I'll do what you have asked me to, but don't delude yourself. Alcohol is a drug, like the sleeping pills, and your husband will only be able to come off it in a clinic."

"Then he smiled slyly at me, "if you want to have a child from a healthy man, I'm available should you need me."

Pig! I hope he was joking. And anyway, he isn't the problem.

I've been deceived. By Antonio, by his mother, by everybody. Someone will have to pay.

August 1986

Antonio has worked out when I'm fertile. He'll only make love to me on those days. On the other days he doesn't even touch me.

I hate him for this. When he climbs on top of me, I feel like shouting: "Why don't you think about Arianna while you're doing it". I just want to get some sort of emotional reaction from him. I won't lie: I would be so happy if he were to cry.

But what would happen if he hit me? He's not a violent man, but as he drinks he could lose control. So it's probably better if I just shut up and put up with it.

The only thing he really cares about is his land, and he has the good sense never to drink in the mornings when he has to oversee the farmhands. He knows full well that his kingdom would crumble immediately should he ever appear drunk in front of the men.

Now that it's summer, I like going with him into the fields to get some air. But I don't even want to think about what'll happen in the winter. The boredom will kill me!

My sister Aurelia is the only one of us who has married a man who works in the city, and she has fun: on Saturdays he takes her dancing, on Sundays to the cinema. How I envy her. I would swap all of this land for a husband who works in a factory: at least I wouldn't have to stay at home all the time. Maybe God's punishing me for having chosen a rich husband: I was only nineteen years old, I could have waited. Waited for true love.

September 5th, 1986

In vino veritas. When Antonio drinks, he opens up more. I fear that the only way I'm going to hear his secrets is by hoping that he gets drunk.

Yesterday evening, he said something very interesting." Eva, I'm thinking of writing my will. If I haven't got any children when I die, I won't leave all the land to you. I'll leave half to you and half to my nephew."

"Your nephew? The one who lives in Bologna?"

"Right. His name is Fabio."

What do I care if I get all the land or only half of it! I'm going to sell it anyway.

"Fine," I replied impassively. "I imagine that's perfectly legal."

"Yes, but there's something else that you should know. When Alfredo left for Bologna, he signed away his share of his inheritance. From my father, I mean. So it all belongs to me, but I don't want it all. When my father died, I tore his will to shreds."

"So from a legal point of view, what's changed?"

"Nothing, in practice. In theory, however should you want to appeal against my will, you would discover that half of my land still belongs to Alfredo, and therefore, to his son, although he doesn't know that yet."

In that moment I had nothing but respect for Antonio's honesty, for his pain, for the suffering caused by having a nephew so far away, and I was sincere when I said: "Antonio, I would never dream of contesting your will. You know what? It would do you good to see your nephew again. Why don't you write to him? Tell him that you want to see him, invite him to spend his holidays here."

"No. I swore that I would never write another letter to, to that address. As long as I live. I'll get a notary to sort it out." There they were, those words uttered with an anguish that came from the bottom of his heart. He would never have said anything had he been sober, and his words brought a lump to my throat. How he suffers.

"Antonio," I continued, "listen to me. Arianna doesn't know that your mother is dead. She might see things differently if she knew."

I saw him wince. "You know nothing about Arianna."

"I know everything. Your mother told me. As it was your mother who was the real villain of the piece, if Arianna knew that she was dead, it might break the silence between you two. Why don't you give it a go? Tell her that you want to see your nephew again!"

Is it against my best interests? I don't care. I'm so bored here, I'd do anything for a bit of company. Antonio seemed to be confused so I continued:

"How old is Fabio?"

"Almost sixteen, I think."

"A good age, he'll be chewing at the bit to get away on his own. You want to see him, don't you?"

87

Antonio seemed to be thinking of something else, he was staring off into the middle distance, but all of a sudden, with an unexpected burst of enthusiasm typical of drunks, he said: "You know what? I'd never thought about it like that before? You're a star. Death of the enemy, end of the war. I must write to my sister-in-law. You know what? I'll write to her immediately."

He headed unsteadily towards the study, and I don't know whether he was capable of writing anything that made any sense. But I'm happy that he's written something because the time had come to put an end to this situation: he couldn't carry on loving a ghost. If Arianna were to ignore his letter for the umpteenth time, maybe Antonio would finally stop loving her and notice me instead.

September 8th

I've discovered how he drinks without me knowing: he hides himself away in his sanctuary. He keeps the room locked, but when I realised that he keeps the key hanging on the landing light, I couldn't resist taking it and going in.

Nothing had changed since the day my mother-in-law showed it to me: there was still a candle burning in front of the photograph of Alfredo, the dead man's belongings on the walls, but now there were also two bottles of alcohol and some glasses on the table.

Antonio's refuge.

Our bedroom must have been Alfredo and Arianna's because my husband had changed all the furniture, the curtains, even the colour of the walls, to cancel out the memories. Everything was brand new for us. There's also a room fitted out for a child: the child that we will never have. It must have been Fabio's room. Antonio's not changed anything in that room; there's even an old teddy bear on the bed.

I'm being suffocated by the atmosphere in this house haunted by dead people. I need something new to distract me.

I must ask Antonio to let me help with the grape harvest; at least it'll give me something to do.

September 9th

It wasn't easy convincing him. At first he said, "It's the farmhands who collect the grapes, not the wife of the farmer. My mother never did and neither..."

He stopped himself. He never talks about the other signora Altavilla. I wonder whether he's actually forgotten he's written to her.

"What harm can it do?" I asked. "I like the grape harvest. I used to help my father when I was seven. Tina used to give us a hand too."

Any reference to Tina makes Antonio's eyes light up. Heaven knows why, he was never in love with her.

"But you're only just married. You could be ten days pregnant and not know yet. Any movement could hurt the baby."

"If that's the real reason why I can't help out in the grapevines, then let me put your mind at rest. I'm not pregnant."

The disappointment was written all over his face. Is it possible that he just wants a son or a daughter from me, and nothing more?

In the end he did let me help with the grape harvest, and every now and then he looked at my stomach as if he was trying to convince himself that it really was flat. What an idiot! If I were in the initial stages of pregnancy, I wouldn't be showing yet.

The young farmhands stared at me, sometimes with anger,

sometimes with lust, but my husband didn't notice, or did he just not care? I would have preferred him to be jealous, and say to them: *Hey! What are you looking at?*

I'm twenty years old, and I like knowing that other men desire me. My husband is the only man who never looks at me like that. What I have done to deserve such a dreadful fate?

I do care about him, and I have tried to be a good wife. But if I never feel loved, who knows what might happen one day.

October 5th

Incredible news: a letter's arrived from Arianna!

He didn't even have the courage to open it. When I came into the study, he was turning it over and over in his hands and his face was white, as if he had just seen a ghost.

"What's the matter, Antonio?"

"Nothing."

"What's in the letter? Bad news?"

"I don't know. I haven't read it. It's from my sister-in-law."

My heartbeat quickened. Why was I so nervous for him?

"Fine," I said. "I should imagine you'll want to be left alone to read it."

"No. Please Eva, you read it. Out loud."

He gave me the envelope and it was as if he was putting my loyalty to the test. It was the first time in our marriage that he had entrusted me with anything. There was real terror in his eyes; he needed someone by his side.

Without saying anything, I took the letter and started to read:

"Dear Antonio, I think your request to see Fabio is legitimate (oh Lord, only a law graduate would use such words) and your letter has arrived at a most opportune moment. After failing his first year of high school, Fabio has decided not to return to full time education, and we don't know what he wants to do when he grows up. At this point it would be a blessing if he were to discover a passion for farming or something along those lines. You could train him in your profession, and if the boy were to show an interest in the land, I would buy him an estate in the north: I know very well that he has lost the rights to his father's land. Money is no object for me because I'm now married to a rich man…"

"What?" shouted Antonio when he heard this, and I stopped reading.

He started shaking and I knew full well why. Very sweetly I asked: "Don't you want to hear the rest?"

After a long wait, he made a sign for me to continue.

"…a rich man who's in politics and now my surname is Fiorentini. I moved house five years ago, but your letters arrived punctually at my parent's house and I always got them. I wanted you to know that. I can send your nephew whenever you want, seeing that he's not at school. Let me know when it would be convenient for you. Arianna."

After having read the letter I said: "Your sister-in-law's done all right for herself. Now she's got herself another husband it suits her to keep her son out of the picture for a while. He probably hates his stepfather. "

"How could she!" murmured Antonio, shocked.

"Are you telling me that you're surprised? She was so young when her first husband died. She couldn't spend the next fifty years in mourning."

"It wasn't just anybody!" he screamed. "It was my brother!"

"Are you trying to say that he was special? Or that she should have fought for justice for him? Obviously she didn't love him as much as you thought she did."

A couple of tears rolled down his cheeks when he heard my words. They were not the crocodile tears of a drunkard but tears of pain, and God only knows how sorry I was.

The moment I had been waiting for had arrived, the

moment to hug Antonio, to make him feel my warmth, to make him understand that I was the woman for him! But I couldn't. Faced with such desperation, I felt like crying too.

"Why?" I cried. "Why didn't you do something if you loved her so much? She was a widow, she didn't belong to anyone!"

"She was Alfredo's, she should have been faithful to him. Fabio can't accept that surrogate father, whoever he is. I'll have him, I'll have the boy. Arianna's not worthy of him!"

He covered his face with his hands. Is it really over? He doesn't love that woman anymore?

I don't believe it. I'll never believe it. I wanted to scream: idiot, you've got a beautiful twenty year old wife and you're tearing yourself to pieces over an old slag who left you fifteen years ago! She didn't even know how to love your brother and her son. What chance did you have?

But how could I shout at a man who was desperate, who was so ashamed for having cried in front of me?

November 5th

It's been raining hard all day and any sort of work on the land is out of the question. Antonio has disappeared; I imagine he's holed up in his room, drinking. Would it have been too much to ask to spend a bit of time with his wife?

Now I really regret marrying him. I thought I was a missionary, ready to conquer the heart of a man that was full of mysteries and anguish! I was wrong. I haven't got a missionary's spirit. I want to enjoy myself, see new people!

I thought that the party organised to introduce us was just a taste of the bright and happy life that awaited me, but I haven't worn a party dress since! Then mourning started for donna Elena, but four months have passed since her death and it feels like the mourning period has gone on for ever. In this house you breath mourning, you eat mourning!

I know that I could stop taking the birth control pills and bring a child into the world, which certainly would liven things up a bit, but it's too risky: a child by Antonio might not be healthy. What would happen if I ever did decide to make my escape, a child would chain me to this place. What if Antonio, who's already in a bad way, were to die young?

Picture the scene: I'm a widow with an adolescent son and I ask him: *Sweetheart, shall we sell this land and move to the city?* But the boy, a farmer like his father, stares at me wide eyed and replies: *Are you mad Mama? This is our land, this is where we belong.*

Speaking of boys: Antonio's nephew arrives tomorrow. He's coming from a modern city and is used to a completely different way of life. He certainly won't sit in the living room doing nothing. He might turn out to be an ally, someone to pass the time with, although I'm sure he'll find a group of friends that are too young for me and I'll be left out.

No, I couldn't go out with a group of sixteen year olds. Fabio turns sixteen the day after tomorrow. Antonio telegraphed Arianna: "Send him to me for his birthday."

As if Arianna isn't capable of organising a party for her son. I think I know what Antonio wants to do.

He will lavish on the boy all the love he had for his parents. Why should I give my husband a son? Fabio's the ideal heir.

I'll have to be careful though. In this house, it will be Fabio who will get anything he wants, not me.

However, seeing that he's only a boy, and therefore malleable, I could teach him to want what I want. I won't just stand there and watch, that's for sure.

The famous nephew has arrived. Antonio went to get him at the station at nine o'clock this morning: luckily at that hour he's always sober, so he was fit to drive a car.

Fabio is such a handsome boy; he looks vaguely like the old photo of Alfredo, although Antonio says that he's got Arianna's blue eyes. My husband should be happy, but I haven't seen him smile once. It's as though he's lost the ability to be happy.

Or maybe he's understood that Fabio isn't in the least bit interested in the farm. At the table, Antonio said: "I want to buy you something nice for your birthday. Would you like a horse?"

Fabio looked at him as though he had just been offered a piece of scrap metal, then he replied, "Thank you Uncle but I wouldn't want to put you to any trouble."

"But I've got to get you a present! That's why I asked you to come here."

"I don't know how to ride, but if it's that important to you, a bit of cash wouldn't go amiss."

You're right, you don't know how to ride a horse. But you'll soon learn, my wife will teach you. She's a fantastic horsewoman."

But Fabio seemed more irritated than happy and continued eating without replying.

"So you would like some money, then. What were you thinking of buying?" I asked.

"I don't know, but I'll have to go into town sooner or later, to the cinema or somewhere like that. Is there a coach that goes into Palermo from here?"

"Of course there is!" I replied. "I use it all the time because I don't drive. Do you fancy coming with me one of these days. We could go for a wander if you like?"

"I'd love to."

Antonio seemed to be against the idea and glared at me. Serves him right. But after we had finished lunch, he started again: "Fabio do you want to take a nap? I want to show you the farm this afternoon and you'll need plenty of energy."

The young man looked at me as though he was asking for my help, so I said: "Antonio, the tour of the farm can wait until tomorrow. They say the weather's going to get worse. We'll spend this afternoon chatting to your nephew, to get to know him better."

Luckily I was right about the weather: it began to pour down soon after lunch, and the outing was called off. I showed Fabio the house, and he didn't show any emotion whatsoever when he saw the room where he slept as baby: he doesn't remember anything of that period. Antonio, disappointed, had disappeared, leaving me alone with the boy. I took advantage of his absence to have a word and said: "Fabio, your uncle wanted you to fall in love with the land. If you don't give a damn about it, don't let on. It would be a mistake. Pretend that you like it, believe me, it's in your best interests."

He stared at me with a certain diffidence. Obviously he thought it odd that an aunt to whom he had never spoken before was giving him advice.

"I don't know what I think about the farm yet," he replied. "I might like it."

"Fine. But remember your uncle is crazy about this land and he is well-disposed to all those who are like him. If you want to win his trust, compliment him on his livestock and he won't mind if you go into the city for a few drinks every now and then."

This time he smiled at me for he knows he's found an ally. But I didn't say those things to help him: I wanted Antonio to think, at least for a time, that the nephew he'd always dreamt of has finally arrived.

I've discovered what makes Fabio tick, and I'm starting to enjoy myself. If anyone is able to liven things up around here, it'll be him.

This morning I got chatting to him after Antonio had shown him the farmstead. All three of us were in the stables, and my husband was asking me to choose a horse that would be suitable for a beginner, when he was called away by one of the workers for something, I don't know what, but it was urgent. I found myself alone with Fabio and I showed him a gentle old nag, saying: - If you mount him, I can guarantee he'll never throw you off. -

"Okay," he replied, without showing any particular signs of enthusiasm.

I wanted to laugh when I saw his face. "Why on earth did you agree to come here?"

"It was my mother's idea."

"And you had to agree to come, even though you didn't really want to?"

"I'm still underage, aren't I?" (You could tell how much it galled him!)

"What's your mother like?"

"Just like all the others."

"You don't want to talk about it, do you?"

"She's ambitious. I was always being left with my grandparents when I was younger and she was slogging away in the office for a promotion. Then she became a manager. She was a manager when she met that, that politician."

You could infer a lot from the tone he used.

"You don't get on with your stepfather, did you?"

"No."

"What did he do to you?"

"He hit me. I didn't deserve it."

I smiled to lighten the mood.

"Are you sure you didn't deserve it?"

"Judge for yourself. If you have an unpleasant stepfather, you do your utmost to stay out of the house as much as possible, right? Not that I did anything particularly bad while I was out, I didn't snatch bags from old ladies or anything like that. But the bastard was out to get me and told my mother that I was keeping bad company. One day she found out that one of my friends had been caught with a couple of joints, but that was nothing to do with me. Do you want to know what my stepfather did? He called me up, furious, he said that I shouldn't be seen with such people, that he was in the running for mayor and that I was tarnishing his reputation! I said: 'You're not my father, you can't choose my friends, and I don't give a damn about your reputation.' And then he hit me."

I bet he's smoked the odd joint, but I wanted to humour him. "Well, I think you're right. He was well out of order even if you were, well, you were rather cheeky."

Fabio smiled and then let slip, "I scared him, the bastard."

"How?"

"I threatened him with a knife. And I said: 'There will be trouble if you try to hit me again.' He was shitting his pants."

"Do you always walk around with a knife in your pocket?"

"Mmm..." His face turned red. "What's wrong with that? In Bologna if you go out in the evening, you must be prepared to defend yourself. There are guys that'll beat you to a pulp for the change in your pocket and then there are the paedophiles."

What are paedophiles? Never heard of them. This boy understands more about life than me. It's because he's really lived, and I haven't.

"Anyway, I'm sure it was that knife that ruined your relationship with the politician. I'm right aren't I? What did he say to you?"

This time Fabio hesitated. He looked upset, as if I'd hit a sore spot. I lowered my voice trying to make my tone more persuasive. "I see. He said something that he shouldn't have, and that was worse than the slap, wasn't it?"

"How do you know?"

"Tell me what he said. It'll be our secret."

When he replied, his voice shook with rage. "I wouldn't have touched him. But when he saw the knife he said, 'You little delinquent, you can tell you're Sicilian!' He had no right to insult me just because I was born here. That's why he hated me. He thought that having a Sicilian stepson, with a father who was killed by the Mafia, brought shame on the family. So I, *we* didn't see each other again after that."

"Did you try to stab him?"

"I tried to. But he dodged out of the way."

Christ! "And your mother," I said, "wasn't she offended too? She was married to a Sicilian!"

"My mother wasn't there. She didn't hear what he said."

"Didn't you tell her?"

"No."

"But didn't you want to explain to her why you pulled a knife on him?"

"It wouldn't have changed anything. She would have believed his version, not mine."

He was telling the truth: I could see his eyes were glistening with tears. I had learnt a lot.

A woman as proud as Arianna, doesn't write to her brother-in-law after fifteen years of complete silence to say: 'Here, if you want my son, take him,' unless it suits her to send him away.

Poor lad, I don't doubt that he's a little hoodlum but in his defence, his mother has obviously neglected him. 'She would have believed him, not me,' and she calls herself a mother?

"And that's why," I concluded, "they sent you on a nice holiday to keep you away from your dear stepfather."

"If he hadn't been up for election, she would have sent me to a youthful offenders' institution. He and his fucking reputation."

"What are you going to do when you go back to Bologna?"

"I don't know."

"Have you ever thought that in two years time you'll be an adult and you can go and live on your own? Your mother is rich, she'll give you a hand financially."

"Yeah, and when she dies, who's going to support me? I couldn't go out to work, I didn't get my diploma."

"Why didn't you stay in school?"

"Because there was such a bad atmosphere at home that I didn't feel like doing anything."

All the pieces of the jigsaw puzzle were falling into place. This boy is a blank canvas and I could make something of him. He doesn't know what he wants yet, but I can show him the way.

"Eva, I've never told anyone this."

"Because you've never had anyone to talk to before," I said soothingly.

"I don't want uncle Antonio to know."

"You can trust me. I won't tell a soul."

What good would come out of telling my husband that Alfredo's son isn't an angel?

Winter hasn't arrived yet. It's still warm enough to stay outside for a couple of hours, so I watch Antonio's pitiful attempts to instil a bit of love for the farm into his nephew. Today, in attempt to see the results of three long weeks of battle, my husband asked Fabio what he thought was the most interesting of all the things he had seen so far.

"The livestock," replied the boy, to please him.

"Why livestock?"

"Because it is the least risky. All it takes is a sudden change in temperature or a parasite, and a harvest is ruined. But to lose all the livestock would take an epidemic and with modern antibiotics, the risks have been greatly reduced."

It seemed that Fabio had learnt his lessons well. Antonio almost smiled.

"So when you have your own farm will you just concentrate on livestock?"

"My own farm?"

"Your mother mentioned it in her letter. She's willing to buy you a farmstead in Romagna. But I wouldn't advise concentrating all your efforts on livestock: it's always better to have two means of support, income from livestock and income from crops. It's also costly to buy the feed for your animals, you'd be better of producing it yourself."

"It's true. You're right," agreed Fabio, but he looked at me as if he to say: 'Enough already, my uncle's driving me crazy.'

"You'll be staying here for a few months won't you?" continued Antonio. "I've still got lots of things to teach you. On the land there is something different to do every month. You'll have to stay twelve months to learn everything."

'I'd rather die!' screamed Fabio's eyes. But my husband hasn't realised yet. He likes teaching so much that he's even cut down on his drinking. He'd rather be sober when he's with the boy, and so far he's managed to avoid being drunk in front of Fabio. But if he's got this strength of will, why doesn't he use it all the time? Why are there still days when he locks himself in that damned room with Alfredo's photo?

December 5th

I was wrong. Antonio's started drinking again, maybe because he sensed that Fabio's taking him for a ride, or perhaps because he tried to ignore the cravings and just wasn't strong enough.

Last night he gave me a terrible fright. We were already in bed when he started:

"I don't like those eyes."

"What eyes?"

"Those there on the wall. I don't like the way they're looking at me."

I sat on the bed. "Antonio you're hallucinating."

"No I'm not. They're blue like Fabio's, two evil eyes, and they are there on the wall staring at me. Get rid of them."

I started to panic because no doctor had ever warned me about this type of episode, and I didn't have any suitable medication in the house. I tried to calm him down, but he continued:

"Get rid of those eyes, make them go away, put a curtain on top of them! Please Eva, please." His cries brought Fabio running to the bedroom.

"What's going on?" he said.

"There's nothing to worry about. Your uncle's pissed."

"On the ceiling!" howled Antonio. "Now that they're on the roof, they're laughing at me from up there!"

The lad was understandably shocked. "What's he talking

about?"

"Take no notice. Now that you're here, you can give me a hand. I have to hang a blanket from the light."

Hang a blanket. He must have thought I was crazy.

"We've got to indulge him, we'll cover what he thinks he can see and then he'll calm down. Will you help me?"

While Fabio and I started to hang the blanket, Antonio muttered: "Who is he? Send him away!"

"Holy crap!" cried the boy. "I've seen some drunks in my time, but none as far gone as he is. That's really shocking!"

"It's not if you think of it as fifteen year bender," I said.

"Fifteen years?" He seemed to be reminded of something.

"He tried to cut down for a few days because you were here, but now he's started to drink again, or he's going through withdrawal symptoms. I don't know, I'm not a doctor."

"Why did he start all those years ago?"

"I'll explain everything in the morning. Now got to bed, Fabio, please."

He left the room visibly shaken. I feel sorry for him, he'll be feeling as if he's always ending up in the midst of the wrong people, but it's too early to tell him the whole truth yet.

The blanket we hung up covered half of the room, and I whispered to my husband, "the wicked eyes have gone. I've got rid of them, okay?"

"Thank you," he slurred, before falling asleep. But I stayed awake for another hour, watching him in case he suffered another attack.

Of all the things that he could have seen, spiders, snakes — why did it have to be his nephew's eyes that terrorised him so?

December 10th

I decorated the Christmas tree today but without the excitement I used to feel when I was younger. The doctor says that Antonio is delirious, and he gave me some pills, which I'd never heard of, but there are some terrible things written in the instructions.

Fabio helped me put up the tree, with much courtesy, but he too seemed to be unexcited by the occasion. I still haven't found anything to arouse his enthusiasm.

"You look worried. Is everything all right?"

"Yes, I just can't decide whether to spend Christmas here or at home."

"Your uncle will definitely want you here. Would you prefer to go back to Bologna?"

"I don't know. All my friends are there so I would enjoy myself more, but the thought of seeing that man again..."

"I see."

I like listening to the lad's secrets. I'm the youngest of seven children, and he's like the younger brother that I never had. He's someone to mother. I would like to mother Antonio too, if he were to open up to me once in a while, but other than that unforgettable day when Arianna's letter arrived, he's kept himself to himself.

"If I could grow to like this place, I would have some good news to give to my mother," said Fabio. "But I can't find anything to get enthusiastic about. If I go home now, what do I tell her? That she should forget about buying me a farm? My stepfather would say: I knew that good for nothing would never do anything worthwhile with his life. Shit, I'd rather die than listen to his comments."

"But what would you like to do when you grow up? If you could do anything you wanted?"

"I would like to have money, and to spend it. Don't laugh, I know that it's the dream of all dossers like me. But there are loads of people who live like that. Take my mother's husband for instance. What do you think he does all day? Nothing:

103

he's got money and he spends it. He got into politics to stop himself dying of boredom."

"How did your 'mother's husband' make his money?"

"Property. Obviously you need some capital to start off with. You buy apartments and then sell them on when their prices rise, then you buy land with planning permission and then you stop. You keep twenty or so apartments to rent out and live off the rent. I've heard these things discussed hundreds of times at home. I'm sure that I will be able to do the odd deal too, if only I had a bit of money. My mother can't give me much. Her savings would only be enough to buy me a small house, which would only give me enough to live on. But I won't get more than that. That shithead's got the money, not her."

"Don't worry. One day you'll have your own money."

"Yeah, right."

"I'm serious." The time had come to tell him about certain things. Forgive me God if I haven't respected the wishes of my husband, but he's a hopeless drunkard and I doubt that my marriage will last much longer. I've got to think about my future. I'm only twenty years old.

"Listen to me Fabio. Your uncle's in a bad way, let's suppose he dies before he gets to fifty. Who will inherit this farm?"

"You and your children. Only you, if you don't have kids."

"Under law, if there aren't any children, Antonio can leave half to whomever he wants."

"Why are you telling me all this?"

"Because you're the other heir. It's in the will."

The boy hadn't expected this. "I don't believe you. What have I done to deserve it?"

"Why do you think you're here? Antonio adored your father, and your father wouldn't have got a crumb of this land from your grandfather. That's why Antonio decided, which I think is correct."

"Correct? You're not even the tiniest bit envious?"

"Fabio, tell me truthfully: what would you do with your piece of land?"

"I would sell it and invest the money in something else."

"There you go. That's the capital you need. You've found it."

Fabio was silent for a second while he thought about what I'd just said. Then the penny dropped.

"That means that you want to sell your part of the land too."

"That's my boy. Can't you see, if I were pregnant, my child would be like Antonio, it would grow up with strong ties to the land, and would try to stop me from selling it. So I'm not going to have any children."

He smiled. "That's a surprise, Eva. I thought you loved the countryside."

"Up to a certain point, yes. I was born in the country, and should I need to breathe fresh country air, I can always go to my parent's farm. But the way I want to live. I don't want to live like your grandmother Elena. Chained to this place for my whole life, winters included, with my nose pressed to the window watching as the months pass, month of pruning, month of threshing, month of sowing, month of harvesting. No, I don't want your grandmother's life."

"What do you really want, Eva?"

"Probably what you want. To live in a city, to go dancing, to go to the cinema. To have money and to spend it. We'll sell this farm, split the proceeds and then it's each to their own. Are you in?"

"Of course I am! But it seems too good to be true. Uncle could stagger on for another fifty years and I'll still be waiting for my inheritance when I'm seventy."

"That maybe true, but before long he won't be capable of

managing his assets anymore. Everything's falling apart. He never used to be drunk in front of the farmhands, but now he does it all the time. In a few months he'll be completely incapable and he'll have to delegate the running of the farm to someone else. Either you or me. If you stay, and pretend that you love the land with all your heart, you could have a power of attorney in your hands when you legally come of age. I know it's too early to make plans, but as you were agonising over whether to go back to Bologna or not, I felt I had to inform you about what will happen, if you stay."

"I'm very grateful that you trusted me enough to tell me this. At the end of the day, you hardly know me." At that moment, he was as serious as an adult. "How do you know that I won't change my mind and become the perfect farmer?"

"Just thinking of you in the fields makes me laugh," I replied. Fabio laughed.

"Oh, Eva! I'm not very good at pretending! Uncle will never fall for it."

"You've got to work at it. No one gets anything in life without making a few sacrifices. I'm also earning my slice, I'm being very patient with Antonio, and I'll be patient 'til the end."

"You're not even the tiniest bit in love with him?"

His question took me by surprise, and I replied truthfully. Maybe I was too honest, seeing as I was talking to a sixteen year old.

"I tried to love him. But he doesn't love me. There's only ever been one woman for him —"

I stopped myself just in time: I can't tell him everything now, I'll wait until he's older. It's dangerous for a child to know that he has power.

"Who?" he asked.

"You don't know her. A woman who died."

"Is that why he drinks?"

"That too. He never got over the assassination of your father."

"Fifteen years on the piss. He wasn't the sort of man to marry. Did you marry him for his money then?"

"No, I swear I didn't. I hoped —" I didn't continue. Fabio would never understand how it torments me. I changed the subject. "Anyway, please show your uncle some respect. He deserves respect."

"Okay, and what else should I do, other than pretend that I'm in love with the farm?"

"Nothing. If you're good, he'll give you what you want. You could start by asking if you can spend Saturday nights in the city."

"But I haven't got a girl to take with me. Would you come?"

"Me?" I said, shocked.

"You're not that old, you're only twenty, and I can pretend I'm eighteen. You said you wanted to have some fun, didn't you?"

What a sweetheart. But I'll ask Antonio first. I won't do anything without his permission.

December 23rd

Fabio's decided to stay. I told Antonio this evening, and I had to work hard to make myself understood. He was staring at the Christmas tree as if it were the first time he had seen it, and muttered: "Does this thingamabob mean that Christmas is coming again? Without Alfredo? I don't want to celebrate anything."

I knew that that evening's alcohol had already been absorbed, but I continued anyway: "Antonio, I need to talk to you about Fabio."

He was lost in his thoughts. "I hate the holidays. Alfredo

107

was the only one who made them bearable."

A crack always appears in his impenetrable soul when he's drunk.

"What did Alfredo do that was so special?"

"He put presents for everybody under the tree and he had us all guess which box was for whom, and we had to guess by reading the poem that was attached to it. How did the last poem he wrote for me go, for his last Christmas here, when he gave me a pair of boots? 'Here's a little something, That is sturdy and robust, For someone who's toiling, Outside in the dust.' Hell, I can't remember the rest. But I must have still got them somewhere, those boots."

He was trying so hard to remember that I felt a sudden burst of tenderness towards him, but it was only for an instance. I could never build a complete picture of Alfredo from the fragments he gives me, so I gave up and continued talking about Fabio.

"It's actually Alfredo's boy that I want to talk to you about."

"Fabio? What's he been up to?"

"Nothing. Why do you say that?"

"You can never be too careful with a twelve-year old —"

"He's sixteen, Antonio! Sixteen for Christ's sake!" Woe is me, the doctor warned me that he could suffer from amnesia later on, but not now. He's going downhill fast.

"Sixteen? You're right. He was born in nineteen seventy. And don't shout at me just because I can't remember one little thing."

"Listen to me. He hates his home. He shakes at the mere mention of going back there. Would you be happy if he were to stay here with us? It would be as if we had adopted him."

"Why should I adopt the boy? I'll have my own children to worry about."

"Do you understand what I'm trying to say? Fabio and his

stepfather hate each other. Do you want to send Alfredo's son back to Bologna, to a man who hates him?"

Alfredo's son. Those words woke him up, and suddenly he was as sober as a judge when he said: "He hasn't said a word to me about all of this."

"He confides in me as if I were his mother. It's obvious that he's been starved of maternal affection."

"He hasn't got a father either, if that's the reason. Why doesn't he treat me like a father? I gave him his bottle when he was a baby."

"Obviously he'll treat you as a father if you let him stay. Do you want him to stay?"

"I've always wanted him here," replied Antonio weakly. I hope he knows what he's letting himself in for because not even I am sure that I'm doing the right thing.

January 3rd, 1987

Fabio's learnt how he's got to behave. I almost laughed this morning when I saw him in a pair of rubber boots and one of his uncle's old raincoats insisting that he wanted to help with the milking. It was freezing cold, but the boy had got up early to show his uncle that he was keen, and Antonio was happy.

Naturally, at lunch, Fabio took advantage of his uncle's good humour to ask him if he could spend the evening at a nightclub in Palermo. Antonio didn't raise any objections and even went as far as to explain the coach times. "On the way back," he said, "be careful not to miss the midnight coach, because it's the last one, and if you do miss it, you'll have to find a hotel for the night."

"I'll get the one at midnight," promised Fabio. "But the real problem is that I haven't got a lira nor a lady to dance with. Could I take Aunt Eva with me?"

"Why yes, of course. Poor girl, I keep her shut away in this house. Go, and have fun."

He even gave us money, and more than was necessary. I'm satisfied. Clearly I would have preferred to be accompanied by a man of twenty five and not a boy. But I'm not complaining.

January 4th

I would have liked to say that last night was wonderful, but it wasn't. It was a nightmare.

To start with, if I were thirty and Fabio twenty-six, you wouldn't notice the age difference, but at the moment it's plain for all to see! I felt like all the people in the pub were watching us, and I was already pretty uncomfortable because I thought they were all laughing at me, when something terrible happened.

There was a young guy there who had his eye on me, and at some point during the evening, he came up to me because he wanted a dance and asked Fabio to step aside. Convention dictates that at this point the current partner moves away for a bit, but Fabio said rudely: "The lady is with me."

The bloke then made the fatal error of laying his hand on my nephew's shoulder and asked again: "I only asked for a turn."

Fabio, who can't bear to be touched, pushed the stranger back saying: "Get your hands off me."

I knew then that it would end badly. The guy didn't have the face of someone who was easily intimidated. "Hey, Junior," he started, "don't you think you're a bit young to keep a babe like this all to yourself. You're still sucking your mother's tit."

"And you eat shit!" Fabio shot back. The other guy grabbed him by the shoulder, forcing him to turn round.

"Careful, you don't know who you're dealing with, little boy."

The other couples had stopped dancing and were starting to move away. It was then that Fabio pulled out a knife.

"Or maybe *you* don't know who you're dealing with."

Some of the girls started to scream. Oh God, the humiliation. I'm out with a boy who walks around armed! I should have known that he would never have been separated from the knife he used to threaten his stepfather with! I suddenly thought about the police, the scandal. Desperation gave me the strength to grab Fabio by the wrist.

"No!" I shouted. "Stop it!"

"Get out of my way, Eva, he needs to be taught a lesson –"

"For Christ's sake!" I screamed, holding his arm. "It's all over if you do! It's all over!"

Anyway, the other guy, who probably wasn't armed and had been relying on his punches to do the necessary damage, had already taken a step back, and the girls' screams had brought the manager running, or maybe it was just a bouncer in a jacket and tie. Before he could open his mouth I said: "Don't worry, we're leaving! We're leaving! And I started to drag my nephew towards the exit."

He tried to resist, but not too much. He could easily have knocked me to the ground if he had wanted to, but at the end of the day it was in his interests to be dragged away. He had frightened his opponent without having to face the unpleasant consequences.

As soon as we outside and alone, I struck the arm that was holding the knife hard: he wasn't expecting it and dropped the weapon with a stifled cry. I picked it up and hurled it as far as I could, saying:

"You animal! You've only just avoided being sent to the young offender's institution in Bologna, do you really want to try the one in Palermo? Do you think it'd be any better?"

He stared at me, his lips trembling with rage and I wondered whether he was wrestling with the urge to hit me.

"You're a cow like my mother," is all he said. Well, now I know what he thinks about his mother.

After having insulted me, he walked off alone to the coach stop. I followed him, but we didn't say a word to each other while we waited for the coach. Two strangers.

We were the only people on the bus other than the driver and another guy who fell asleep two minutes after the coach left. Fabio went to sit on the other side of the coach. He'd taken umbrage at my words but he would eventually realise that I'd got him out of a lot of trouble.

He didn't move away when, ten minutes after we set off, I went to sit next to him. I had stretched out my arm to ruffle his hair, as a sign of peace, but he surprised me by turningtowards me and putting his head on my shoulder, and I heard him

112

stifle a sigh, but it wasn't remorse. He shook with nerves, with suppressed rage; I could feel his desire to kill someone in those tremors. I didn't know what to do, so I stroked his arm to reassure him.

When we were almost home, I realised that he was sleeping like a baby with his head on my shoulder. Incredible. I watched him while he slept, a fallen angel, offended, his eyes covered by his long lashes. I could sense his youth…and I couldn't believe that only half an hour ago, he was on the point of planting a knife into the stomach of someone who was just like him.

January 7th

I can't believe that Fabio resisted the temptation to spend the Epiphany in Bologna. He had told me about all the fun he and his friends have during the holidays, but he stayed here.

He's written a nice letter to his mother, telling her that he's happy here and that he's not been in any "trouble" (liar!), that he likes it here (double liar!), and that he could stay all winter, and beyond.

He's promised to visit his mother at Easter and told her not to worry about him, and so forth.

But if I've understood correctly, Arianna would be more than happy if she never saw her son again.

June 1st

The hot weather's finally arrived. I can spend more time outside and today I must say I enjoyed myself. Antonio had made Fabio responsible for overseeing the sheep sheering, and I, knowing how much these things bore the boy, decided to keep him company. We were sat on the gate of the pen, chatting.

"Let's play a game to pass the time," I suggested "Choose a man who you think is the quickest worker, and I'll choose another one and we'll have a bet — who will sheer the most sheep in an hour?"

"If you really want to," said Fabio. "I'll bet on the blond-haired guy over there."

"I'll go for the little thin one. Check your watch, the hour starts now: it's a quarter past ten."

"And if I win the bet, what will you give me?"

"How about some money?" I said to him. "But you've got nothing to give to me if you lose."

"What's the point in betting if there's nothing at stake," he muttered.

"Okay, then. You come up with a game."

"Fine. Let's do rhymes. One of us says a line and the other has to make up a second line that rhymes with the first."

"But I'm hopeless at rhymes!" I protested.

"It's the easiest thing in the world. Do you want an example?"

"Go on then."

"Promise me you won't be offended."

"Why, is it offensive?"

"No, no but let's say your husband doesn't come out of it very well."

I wouldn't have expected anything less….

"You're making me curious."

He then whispered a couple of lines in my ear that started with 'Uncle Toni loved a cow,' and you can imagine how the rest went. Silly doggerel, but I must admit that I almost died laughing; Fabio has a good ear. I'd heard that his father had the same gift too, but I'm sure that Alfredo used his for more refined means.

I tried to admonish Fabio for his lack of respect for his uncle, but I was laughing more than he was, so much so that

114

I wanted a go. "Listen to this," I said, "I'm going to make up a line and you've got to come up with a second line with the same meter and the same rhyme. Okay?"

"I'll amaze you!" he promised.

He was actually very good. I've forgotten most of the stupid things we came up with, but I do remember a couple. "When Uncle Toni goes to sleep, his snoring makes the angels weep..." Then I tried something more difficult: "And if he were to drink some red?"

Fabio: "He'd end up in a flower bed." We carried on for another half hour, laughing our heads off like silly children. It really was like having a younger brother.

We were still laughing when Antonio came into the pen. He looked surprised when he saw our contorted faces: I was so ashamed, I wished the earth would swallow me whole.

"What are you doing here?" he said. "Signora Altavilla shouldn't been seen in the sheep pen."

"Sorry. I was bored and so I thought I'd keep your nephew company. Did you know that he tells the best jokes?"

The face that my husband made saddened me. His expression wasn't disapproving, no. It looked as though he was thinking that we were two kids and he was just an old man.

"Jokes during work hours!" was all he said. Then he wandered off, swaying, and my heart ached for him.

"Look how he walks," said Fabio. "His legs are about to give way. Not long now, eh?"

"Not long now until what?" I said, suddenly feeling the need to protect Antonio.

"Until he won't be able to oversee anything. He'll take to his bed and amen."

"Don't underestimate him, he won't take to his bed. He loves his land too much to ignore it completely."

"But he's not even capable of doing the accounts."

"That doesn't matter. He's already given them to me. I've been doing them now for about six months," I said.

"You could have told me! Does this dump make a good profit then?"

"You bet it does. It would be a shame to sell it."

Fabio's face clouded over. He remembered my promises very clearly. "You haven't changed your mind, have you?"

"No. Don't worry. We deserve to see more than just sheep being sheered."

"Speaking of money, do you think Uncle will give me a motorbike?"

"Of course. Why don't you ask him?"

"I think I'm asking for too much from him. He already gives me hundred thousand lire every Saturday for the stuff I need."

"He'll get you one, and he'll get you a car when you turn eighteen."

"I think it's odd that he's only generous to me. He's so tight with everyone else. He'll even moan about the price of a straw hat."

"That's got nothing to do with being tight, it's just the way they do things here. The hat seller knows his hat is worth three thousand lire, but he'll ask five thousand because he knows that the customer will try and lower the price. The hat will eventually be sold for three thousand, which is how it should be. But you're not a trader, you're his only nephew."

Fabio nodded to show me that he had understood, but he didn't seem convinced. "Something's not right though."

"Why?"

"Well, I am underage. When my mother gave me money, she wanted to know how I was going to spend it. But Uncle never asks me. Isn't he worried that I'll go and buy drugs or something?"

"He doesn't believe that you are capable of doing anything

wrong."

"Why? Because he worshipped my father? Because my father was perfect so I've got to be perfect too?" He's finally understood. And he still doesn't know the half of it.

"That's exactly right," I replied. I'm not going to tell him about Arianna, I'm not going to let on that he can get anything he wants from Antonio. I don't share my husband's blind faith in him.

I can't forget the feeling of remorse that washed over me as I watched Antonio slink off with his tail between his legs while we laughed at him.

November 28th 1989

The one thing that I'd feared the most has finally happened. Yesterday at lunch, Antonio came in from the fields looking shaky. He opened his mouth to try and tell me something and collapsed onto the floor. A heart attack.

At the moment he's in hospital and the doctor said that he'll make a good recovery as he's only forty years old, but another one could be fatal. I've got to rid this house of all the alcoholic drinks I can find, but I'm under no illusions: as soon as Antonio is out of bed, he'll buy some more. There's nothing wrong with his legs.

"How long will he have to rest for?" I asked.

"As long as possible," was the doctor's answer.

"I'll look after him for as long as it takes, but the farm can't wait," I said. "If you think that he'll be out of action for a while, I'll need a power of attorney to buy and sell animals, materials and all the rest. What do you think?"

"Certainly, the convalescent period won't be short, but you won't find a lawyer who will let your husband sign a power of attorney if he sees that he's suffering. A person must be of sound mind to hand his affairs over to someone else."

I know. The family doctor knows full well that Antonio isn't sober. He would never sign a certificate saying that he was. This infuriated Fabio.

"He'll be around for another hundred years and we'll still be here gathering dust!" he muttered, even though I was the only one who could hear him.

"Calm down, young man. You're only nineteen years old, you can't have everything at once. We'll wait until your uncle is sober, and then we'll ask him if he wants to sign over the running of the farm to us, okay?"

"It'll be the management of the farm he'll give us, not the farm itself. We won't be able to sell it."

"Fabio, don't think that I want to get rid of my husband. As long as he's alive, he'll live here."

"Isn't there anything else we can do? If he really has lost his marbles, we could always lock him away in an institution."

How can he talking about 'locking' his uncle away when he's never shown him anything but love. I could have slapped him.

"Fabio," I said severely, "you'll have your inheritance when he's dead. But as long as he's alive, I'm his wife, and I'll be the one in charge. Is that clear?"

He glared at me, offended.

"Well at least try to remember all the different medicines that he's got to take, and try to make sure he is sober for a couple of days when he gets home. If he doesn't sign a power of attorney, we won't even be able to buy food for the sheep and we'll be heading for disaster before we know it!"

That I can't deny.

December 10th

We've done it. Antonio's home and I've convinced him that

while he's convalescing, Fabio and I should take care of his beloved land. We got a notary to come to the house with a power of attorney. The notary doesn't know Antonio, and as we only showed him the doctor's notes that mentioned the heart attack, he would never have guessed that Antonio was an alcoholic. All he saw was a man who was not yet forty, confined to bed for heart problems, who gave no sign of being in any way mentally impaired.

"Do you, signor Altavilla," he asked him, "want that your wife and your nephew manage the farm until you are fully recovered?"

"Of course I do," replied Antonio. "There's a motor show in December and I need a new tractor, and if I can't go, I'll send my nephew."

The notary didn't raise any objections. And now we have the power of attorney.

I really will slap Fabio one of these days. He just went and called his mother in Bologna, his mother the law graduate, because he wanted to know what legally he could and couldn't do now that he was in possession of a power of attorney. Sell a piece of land? Apparently you can.

This angered me. "Fabio! As long as your uncle is alive, I will never let you sell anything."

"Oh come on. As long as he's alive, he'll see his land stretching as far as the eye can see. If I sold ten thousand metres from the part that borders onto the Picciotto sisters' land, he'd never notice. Do you really believe that he'll ever be strong enough to go riding around the whole farm?"

Little shit. This is the price I'm paying for not wanting to give Antonio a son. An alliance with Fabio.

The price I have to pay for my freedom when God decides the time is right.

Antonio's already forgotten that he's signed the power of attorney!

This morning he wanted to get up and go to the farm machinery show, and I had a struggle getting him to stay in bed.

"I've got to buy a tractor!"

"Fabio will go. Don't forget, he's got a power of attorney."

"What power of attorney?"

"Oh, Christ Almighty. The one you signed the other day."

"If you say so. But do you think Fabio knows how to recognise a good tractor?"

"Of course he does. He has learned everything he knows from you."

"Does he know how much he's got to spend? Why don't you go with him?"

"I've got to stay with you. Otherwise you'll get up and go and look for something to drink!"

"That'll happen sooner or later. I can't stay in bed forever. I'm only thirty-nine years old!"

"I'll watch you night and day."

He lay back down and sighed. "You deserve a better husband," he said suddenly.

I could have shouted: *No! No Antonio, I'm not the saint you think I am. I'm just a nurse who's only doing her job because she gets paid. I'm sorry that it's come to this. If you could have cancelled out your memories with passion for me instead of alcohol, maybe I could have loved you.*

Maybe, but it doesn't matter now. It's too late.

Last night. Damned night.

It was all Antonio's fault. It was around ten o'clock when he started to scare me. He was suffering from the drugs and had got up to look for something to drink, and in his desperation started throwing everything into the air, screaming like a madman all the while. When I rushed over to try and calm him down, he accused me of being a whore and tried to hit me. He had never been violent towards me before, and I was scared because I was on my own: Fabio was at the motor show. I telephoned for my brother Agostino who came immediately, and helped me hold Antonio down when I gave him one of the injections prescribed by the doctor. Christ, I was afraid he would have another heart attack, but the injection calmed him down, and after a few minutes he fell asleep.

It was midnight. My brother had gone home, and I was sat on the sofa, trembling and sobbing like a baby. Fabio, I thought, where are you? It seems ridiculous, but in that moment I missed that little rascal. I was also worried: it was late and now that he's got his own car and is no longer reliant on the coach, there's no reason why he would have to stay overnight in the city. If he's not home by midnight, the first thing that comes to mind is a road accident. The motor show doesn't go on that late!

I waited up for him, a thick dressing gown over my night dress, like a mother waiting for her reprobate son. He came back at five past one, and I was so angry with him that I would have beaten the living daylights out of him had I not noticed that he too was upset.

"Fabio! What happened?"

"I'm an idiot. I lost money."

I breathed a sigh of relief. At that moment, money was the last thing I cared about, I was so grateful to him for having returned home so that I would no longer be alone with a madman.

" Well," I said, trying to control my voice, "didn't you buy anything?"

"Yes. Luckily, I'd already paid for the tractor, it's being delivered tomorrow, but I had five thousand lire left and I lost it."

Nothing serious. I was beginning to find it easier to breathe. "Did it fall out of your pocket?"

"I could tell you it did, but it would be a lie and I wouldn't know how to lie to you. I was fleeced by a girl. She was making eyes at me, a pretty girl at the show. I invited for a coffee at the bar, and she said that if I wanted to do something else, she was willing. So I took her to a motel, I paid for a room and then — I don't remember anything else. That whore must have slipped something into my drink. I was woken up by someone banging the door of the next room, the girl had disappeared, and with her my money. Why are you laughing?"

I was laughing my head off. I thought it was hilarious that someone like Fabio could have fallen for one of the oldest tricks in the book. Maybe he just assumed that she was interested in him because he was so handsome. He's grown into such a good-looking guy that the girls chase after him, just as they chased after his father, if Tina's stories are to be believed. The girl at the show wasn't mesmerised by his beautiful eyes though, oh no. She knew what she was doing.

"These things happen at your age," I said. "That little madam saw you buying things at the show and knew you had money on you. Don't worry: you won't fall for it a second time."

"Aren't you angry?"

"No."

"But if my uncle were to find out that I go with whores, he'll take the power of attorney away from me."

"And who's going to tell him? Me?"

"I was seen, Eva. Your brother-in-law was at the show, Tina's husband. He was buying a threshing machine. And he saw me leave with the girl on my arm."

"How terrible!" I said sarcastically.

"Don't underestimate the trouble I could be in. Tina comes round every now and then."

"Why are you worried about her? She talks, but your uncle doesn't listen to her. He's in a world of his own. If only you knew what he did this evening, no, it doesn't matter."

I was still too shaken to re-live the moment when Antonio tried to attack me. I was scared I was going to cry, and the last thing I wanted was Fabio to see me as a vulnerable woman. He's got to see me as strong and decisive, otherwise I will no longer be able to dominate him.

"Eva, I know what my uncle's condition is, but he does have days when he is completely sober, like the day when he signed the power of attorney," said Fabio, worried.

"I can assure you that he would never punish you, not if even if you went with all the whores in Italy."

"I don't believe you. Why am I so special?"

Then I realised that the moment had come to tell him. The man had been following me for three years now, as if he were blindfolded and I were guiding him along an unknown street. He's nineteen years old; it was time to take the blindfold off.

"Have you ever seen the shrine of the house?"

"What shrine?"

"It's in a room that only Antonio's allowed to enter, but at the moment he's dead to the world, so I can show it to you."

I took the key that was hidden in the landing light and I opened the secret room. Nothing had changed since the last time I was there. Alfredo's photo, his things hanging from the walls, the candle. How come the candle was lit? Obviously

Antonio got out of bed when my back was turned. He's capable of forgetting everything but his brother.

"This is where your father and uncle slept when they were boys. Now Antonio locks himself in this room to drink and torment himself. He'll be asking himself where the alcohol has gone: I got rid of it."

Fabio was looking around with the same air of perplexity that I would have had when my mother-in-law showed me the room. "What's with candle? Has my father been canonised without me knowing?"

"Don't laugh Fabio. Your uncle was strange even before he started drinking. Your father was his idol, but Antonio was in love with your mother. That's the woman he's always loved — at least in his dreams. He's tortured himself for his whole life over this, and the result is that you are sacred to him. You are the son of the only two people that he has ever loved, and you're sacred. Now do you understand?"

"My mother? It can't be true. She's never said a word to me about it!"

"She would have known, because in sending you here she knew she was giving you a future. She might have married a bastard, but she's will always be your mother, and she sent you to a place where she knew that you would be treated like a prince."

"So this is the big secret — that has turned my uncle into a wreck?"

How could I have expected that he would understand? There's something so hard about him. He wouldn't be capable of suffering from a guilty conscience. I didn't reply.

"Eva, did you know all of this when you married him?"

"Yes. Your grandmother told me."

"So why did you agree to marry him?"

"I hoped I could make him fall in love with me. I was young, beautiful..."

My voice started to shake and Fabio sensed my disappointment. That wasn't supposed to happen. I didn't want him to pity me.

"So you never did manage to make him forget my mother?"

"No. Never."

"And your marriage?"

"All he wanted was a son. Maybe he would have been able to love his child, but he's not able to love me. And now if there is one person that he's capable of loving unconditionally — it's you."

As far as I was concerned the conversation should have stopped right there, but Fabio obviously thought otherwise.

"Poor Eva," he said sweetly, laying his hand on the top of my breast, which was peeking out over the neckline of my night dress. His touch was expert and made me shiver. No one had ever touched me like that before.

"Leave me alone," I said. "That little tramp at the show has obviously aroused you, but don't go thinking that you can take it out on me! Go to bed. The fun's over."

"Go to bed? That's exactly what I intend to do," he said impudently, moving his hands lower and lower.

"Stop it Fabio. We may be partners but this was never part of my plans. You're only a boy."

"Are you sure about that?"

I was sure up until two hours ago. But now everything's changed. It felt as though he had been touching women for at least twenty years. When he put his hand between my thighs, I almost screamed, and that was when I should have punched him on the nose, but I didn't dare to. That hot hand, that hand that knew where to go, was irresistible.

Seeing that I wasn't resisting, he lifted me up and in a second I was on Alfredo's sacred bed.

"No, please!" I protested weakly.

"You won't regret it. Since my uncle doesn't know how to treat a beautiful woman like yourself, you've got a lot to learn. Lingerie? You shouldn't wear panties under your night dress," he said, sliding them down. "My mother never wore them."

"How do you know that?"

"I spied on her, every now and then."

"You're a pig." I stiffened as the image of a twelve year-old boy who spied on his mother through the keyhole appeared before my eyes.

"What are you making all this fuss for?" he asked. "You wanted it as much as I did. You knew full well that sooner or later we would have done it."

"That's not true..."

Maybe I had always been attracted to him and was waiting until he grew up, without noticing that he was already grown. He had caught me when I was at my most vulnerable after what had happened that damned evening. And anyway, how was I to know that he would have pushed me onto that bed...

But then I glanced at Alfredo's photo and I got the terrible sensation that I was desecrating a shrine.

"Fabio, no!" I screamed. "Not in *this* room!"

He followed my eyes to the shrine and laughed.

"You're not superstitious, are you?"

He held me down and I closed my eyes, surrendering myself to him. No, there isn't a shrine in the world that he wasn't capable of defiling. I didn't want Alfredo to be watching me while his son did things to me. God forgive me, I shut my eyes and I let myself go, I let myself go, pushing the image of Antonio who swayed pitifully while he was trying to hit me, out of my head, repeating to myself that it wasn't my fault, seeking refuge in the tremors that rose from my crotch and snaked around my waist.

An orgasm. Now I know what it is.

126

December 16th

My lover. I find it hard to believe that he is the same boy who made me laugh with his dirty doggerel while we sat on the gate of the sheep pen. The boy I considered to be my younger brother, my business partner, and who knows what else. But what's done is done. I've got to be careful, because I don't trust him, even if sexually he drives me crazy. I haven't forgotten the boy who pulls a knife out the minute someone pisses him off.

I mustn't forget that I'm older than he is, that he's got hundreds of girls chasing him, and that he'll leave me as soon as I've served my purpose. Certainly, as long as my husband is alive, he needs me.

April 10th, 1990

It looks as though Antonio's health is improving. He doesn't eat much and it's a miracle if he manages to stand up for more than a couple of minutes, but his love for his land pushes him out into the fields to oversee the farmhands: he takes a chair with him and sits there, watching them. The doctor says that the spring air is good for him, and who are we to argue.

His employees respect their boss who refuses to abandon his empire, despite being weakened by a heart attack. Many of them are older than he is; they were there when he was born and they know how much he loves the land. None of them would ever respond rudely to any of his requests, no matter how strange they were.

However Fabio's young age is turning out to be a problem. They don't take a boy of nineteen seriously whatever he does. Notwithstanding the power of attorney, and the fact that he's learnt how to behave like the perfect country gentleman, the farmhands just don't respect him. Maybe these old men understand that he's not like Antonio, but whatever the reason, unpleasant incidents still occur.

Yesterday, Fabio pissed off a labourer who was smoking, and he was right to do so — a cigarette butt could set fire to hectares of land.

But the old man replied: "What's up, little boy, are you jealous because your parents don't let you smoke?"

When he heard those words, Fabio went for him and punched him in the face, and now the farmhand wants to report him to the police, but I put him straight.

"You could have been fired for smoking during work hours," I told him. "Go back to work and give thanks to God that you've still got a job."

"I can't work with people who don't respect me!" he shouted.

"And I can't do anything more than what I've just done."

"We could be the masters of this land, but all we've got is this power of attorney. Your husband could sign it over to us."

"I really do hope that you're joking. Who's going to ask Antonio to hand everything over, now that his health's improving?"

"Right. He's feeling better. What a disaster!"

I don't know what he meant, but I don't like his words. Neither do I like the fact that he hasn't touched me. Not even a caress.

When Antonio ignored me in the weeks when I wasn't fertile, I was angry. But if Fabio neglects me, it hurts. Why?

I don't know what passion is. I hope it's not what I feel for Fabio. For if this is passion, it hurts. It hurts so much.

After lunch today, I confronted my nephew:

"You said that the improving health of your uncle was a disaster. I want to know what you meant. Do you want to kill him?"

Fabio's eyes danced.

"Wow. Do you think I'm a murderer?"

"I want to know what you want, from him and from me."

"And I don't understand what you want Eva."

Antonio was napping so we were alone at the table. Fabio got up, stood behind me and started to delicately massage my shoulders. He must have felt my pleasure at his touch, for he started to stroke my neck and ears with his tongue, but without kissing me, as if he wanted to kill me with desire.

"Is this what you want? Say it. Do you want it or not?"

I couldn't reply. I was trembling.

"...or do you want your husband, lovingly cared for, to live until he's a hundred? You said that it was the fate of every signora Altavilla to wait with her nose pressed against the window, watching as the harvest month, the threshing month and the sowing month passed. Those were your exact words weren't they? That you didn't want that?"

"Yes."

"But now you've changed your mind."

"No Fabio, I haven't changed my mind."

"Well that'll be your life if your husband lives for another fifty years."

"For Christ's sake Fabio, what are you asking me to do?"

"Nothing. Mother Nature knows what to do. Why don't you let nature take its course? -

"I don't understand."

When I said that he moved away from me. "I know that

129

you've taken the car keys away from him. You had no right to."

"But he's not capable of driving!" I protested. "He'll have an accident! And if he manages to leave the farm, he'll be off buying alcohol."

"You're protecting him from himself, Eva. And that's not down to you. That's all I'm trying to say."

"I promised the doctor that I would make sure that he didn't buy any alcohol."

"Couldn't you lose track of him once in a while?"

Now I understand. Fabio is seriously evil. But what alternative have I got?

"Fabio, please. Don't make me do something bad."

"There's nothing wrong in giving the poor devil his car keys back. Let him go."

"You want him dead!"

"So are you telling me that you want him to live for another fifty years? You'd rather not live in the city and enjoy yourself, meet new people, and all the other things that you plan on doing. And you don't even want me, sweetheart. Think about it. You've got lots of time to think about it."

He left the room and all of a sudden I felt chilled to the bone. Chilled in April.

Forgive me God. Tomorrow I'll tell Antonio that as he's feeling better, he can use the car.

May 5th

Yesterday I pretended not to notice that my husband was drunk. Apparently this is the price I have to pay to get Fabio back. This morning, he did something that surprised me.

He came into my bathroom while I was in the bath with foam up to my neck, and used the toilet as if he hadn't noticed me lying there.

"Hey!" I shouted . "What are you doing?"

"Isn't it obvious? Would you rather I faced you, so you can get a better look?"

The cheek! I was already aroused.

"Can't you see that this bathroom is being used? There are another two in this house!"

"This one was the closest."

He turned round and I saw the expression on his face. The merry face of the boy who made up scurrilous rhymes. The boy that I adore.

"What can I do to make it up to you? Shall I wash your back?"

"Done."

He took of his shirt and I thought it was because he didn't want to get it wet, but then he took everything else off too.

"What are you doing?" I said. "I'm not in the mood for a foam fight!"

"I'm sure you're not. You're a serious woman. But I'm just a boy and I want to play."

"Oh, no."

"Oh, yes —"

I melted in front of his nude body. His chest was well defined and smooth, his thighs streamlined. I can well believe that women were crazy about his father if he was as well made as his son.

In a second he was in the tub, as agile as a cat, and was on top of me. From the expression on my face, he must have understood that I was ready, that there was no need for foreplay. He penetrated me immediately, but then he stopped and we stayed where we were, our eyes locked.

He wasn't moving, he didn't want to give me any pleasure; he was obviously waiting for something.

"What do you want?" I whispered.

"You, Eva, what do you want?"

"Enough of this silly conversation."

He laughed and with an upward thrust, almost made me scream.

"Don't you think that your husband drinks a little too much?" he said suddenly.

"So what? I don't want talk about him."

"Where does he keep his liquor?"

"In the room with the photo of your fa —"

Another thrust. "Wrong answer, darling."

"Why?"

"If the doctor asks you why Antonio has started drinking again, what are you going to say to him?"

"I don't know."

"Now you're talking."

He was moving gently inside me, licking the soap off my breasts. I didn't know that it was possible to have an orgasm in water. But rather than abandoning himself to pleasure, he continued.

"You don't know where Antonio keeps the keys to that room. You don't know, okay?"

"Fine — Oooh!"

I finally relaxed for a moment and I stared at my lover with astonishment. "Who on earth taught you to do those things? You were only sixteen when you came to live here."

"So what? I've been having sex since I was fifteen. My friends bought me women."

"You took lessons from whores? That's disgusting."

"Do you want to be shocked, or do you want to learn a couple of other things?"

He started again and the water in the bath spilled out everywhere. I dare not contemplate what the housekeeper will think when she cleans the bathroom.

I'm sure I dug my fingernails into his shoulder when I felt my second orgasm rise up inside me, but he didn't say anything. That was the moment when I realised that I could never live my life without — without this.

"Don't leave me," I begged. I shouldn't have said anything, but I couldn't stop myself.

"What?" The pleasure he derived from making me say those words again was plain to see.

"Why should I ever want to leave you? You're so beautiful! I'm sure I could have a sixteen year old if I wanted, but she would never be as beautiful as you. And anyway, we're partners. I could marry you."

"Marry me? Are you crazy?"

"After we've buried my uncle, obviously."

"No one marries the widow of their uncle here in Sicily. It's seen as a sort of incest."

"What do you care about Sicily? When we sell the land, we can go and live wherever we want. Do you prefer Bologna, Rome or Milan? If we go somewhere else you won't be my uncle's widow, you'll just be my wife. I'll show you how to have a good time."

I didn't say anything. That was my dream.

"You're still thinking of selling everything, aren't you?" he asked.

"Yes."

Having got what he wanted he climbed out of the bath and slipped on my bathrobe. My bathrobe.

"Okay. All I would need is your permission to start immediately," he said.

"What are you talking about?"

"Do you remember that ten thousand metre squared piece of land at the edge, where uncle never goes?"

"You can't sell it while he's alive!"

133

"Forget about the power of attorney. And anyway, he'd never notice."

"But that piece of land is pasture. That's where the sheep go to graze."

"Who cares about the sheep. If they haven't got enough grazing, we can buy them sheep feed."

"Antonio's always been against using feed that isn't natural," I protested.

"I don't think you understand sweetheart. He's not in charge anymore."

I was angry. He'd only done me in the bath to get what he wanted.

"Why are you so obsessed with that piece of land?" I asked eventually.

"Because I've found a buyer. He's going to build eight villas, each one surrounded by a thousand metres of land. There's a shed load of money to be made."

"When did find the time to organise all of this?"

"Never underestimate me, Eva."

Who would ever do that? It would be a huge mistake.

It was only when I muttered, "We'll talk about this another time," that he gave me my bathrobe back and started to get dressed.

July 2nd

I know that I've got to do more for Antonio. I hardly do anything for him anymore because I don't want to annoy Fabio, and I hate seeing him angry. But my husband's suffering will be on my conscience for the rest of my life.

It's obvious that he's drinking. He's drunk in front of his employees now, and he'll soon lose their respect. Yesterday he wanted to treat a cow's injured hoof, but his hands shook so much that a kind herdsman said "Let me do that," and it took him two seconds to pull the bandage off Antonio's finger and wrap it around the injured hoof. Nobody said anything but my husband's expression grieved me because in that moment he knew that he was useless. So what did he do? He drank some more to blot out the pain!

This morning he saw cockroaches. He saw them in the living room and tried to stamp on them with his boots, screaming and running around far too quickly for a man in his delicate condition. He often lost his balance and fell onto an armchair or a sofa, but he immediately got back up again to crush some more. He then got a huge cushion and held it down on the floor shouting:

"Eva, help me! You've got to help me kill them, they're everywhere!"

It was a terrible scene. I knew it was caused by the DTs and that I should give him an injection, but in that moment I was paralysed by panic. It was only when my nephew entered that I felt able to take control of the situation.

"Fabio," I said, "I've got to give him an injection, can you help me keep him still?"

He stared at me blankly, but I went to prepare the injection anyway. When I returned with the syringe, my husband had climbed up onto a table to escape from the insects, and Fabio was smiling as though he was watching an Oliver and Hardy film.

"Keep him still!" I shouted. "Can't you at least do that? It won't make him live any longer; it'll just make him sleep! Help me!"

I really thought that the boy would refuse. But he gently held his uncle and I gave him the injection.

Fabio didn't say anything while I was doing it: he only let him go when he felt the man's muscles relax, and Antonio collapsed into my arms.

"Don't worry," I whispered to him. "It's me. Eva. You've killed all the cockroaches. They're all dead."

I stroked his hair, overcome by pity and remorse, until he slept. Then I burst into tears, sat there on the sofa and clutching that broken man to me.

I was crying and I would have liked Fabio to console me, but he stared at me as though I disgusted him and left the room.

Why?

September 20th

Antonio doesn't go out much anymore. The last time he tried to drive the car he was drunk and crashed into a tree so they took his licence away.

He stays a home, not saying much, and when he wants to get a breath of fresh air, he goes out into the fields, but not more than a thousand metres from the house. He doesn't get to see much of his land anymore, and Fabio has started to talk about selling the strip of land that borders onto the Picciotto farm.

That boy wants too much too fast. He's even brought the eventual buyer here to start talks. He has a name that I don't like: Vincenzo Messina.

I must have heard of him before, when I was younger. His name was linked to a scandal or something like that.

It could be a case of coincidence, there must be at least thirty people in Palermo with the same name, but I can't shake off this feeling of unease. What if he's a cousin? The apple never falls far from the tree. If one's bad, they'll all be bad.

Of all the millions of people in the world, why did Fabio have to choose Vincenzo Messina? What happens if he promises him a certain price, then only gives him half, or he screws him over in some way?

I'll do a bit of digging. I could ask my sister Tina. She's older than me, so she'll remember the old scandals. But I can't tell her that Fabio's thinking about selling a piece of land. What should I say? I could say that Fabio has lost a hundred thousand lire playing poker with this guy.

Yes, I think that'll work. If Tina does know anything about this signor Messina, she'll tell me.

September 22nd

The information I got from Tina was terrible, and I wanted to warn Fabio, but I was too late; he was already in the study with him.

I went in and I saw Vincenzo Messina. He was over fifty years old, stocky, and looked at everyone as though he was the master of all he surveyed, the type of man that I detest. Talks had already started.

"So the villas will be two storeys high?" Fabio was saying. "And how many can you get on one hectare?"

"About ten. So if you sell me three hectares, I'll be able to build thirty villas."

"Are you sure you'll get permission to build? With all this talk about planning regulations and limiting the number of new houses built?"

He roared with laughter. "You shouldn't be worrying about these kinds of things. Vincenzo Messina has been worked in the building industry for over twenty years, and he's never had any problems getting authorisation."

What a nice man. Flaunting his connections with the Mafia. I couldn't stay silent any longer.

"Fabio, why are you talking about selling three hectares? We agreed on one, didn't we?"

"Eva, we've got two hundred hectares! What difference does it make if we sell one or three?"

"There's the question of the sheep that won't have any grazing. Couldn't we talk about it for a moment in private?"

I rolled my eyes at him to make him understand. I couldn't say "get rid of this criminal" in front of him. But Fabio didn't understand, or he pretended to not understand. He turned back to Messina.

"If you can guarantee that thirty villas will be built, and that you'll sell ten to me, I will sell you the three hectares," he continued.

"Sell ten villas to you? You didn't mention that before."

"These are my conditions," Fabio insisted. What a face he made, that *Mafioso*. It was the face of a person who isn't used to having to accept conditions.

"Could I ask why, Signor Altavilla?"

"So that I will get a personal income from the rent of ten villas. There are lots of people who want to vacation round here."

"I'm not saying that you haven't got a good head for business on you, young man, but I've already got ten buyers lined up for ten villas."

"It just means that some of these people will have to wait for another couple of years. When my uncle dies, I'll be in a position to sell you all the land you need."

"And if I'm not willing to accept your terms?"

"I'll sell the land to someone else," Fabio replied. "I've got plenty of buyers lined up too."

He's brave. He's standing up to a man who's capable of coming back tonight and setting the farm afire. I admired Fabio in that moment, despite everything. Messina though was thinking about the future — all that land! I'm sure that's why he replied: "Very well. You can have ten villas."

"You'll have to put it in writing for the notary."

"If it's that important to you. But Vincenzo Messina only gives his word."

"And I have a predilection for words that are written down on paper."

It wasn't so much a smile that Messina gave Fabio, but a snarl. "You can tell that you come from the north," he commented. "No Sicilian would have dared speak to me like that."

"How ironic!" said Fabio, glancing over at me with sparkling eyes, "When I lived in the north, everyone said 'you can tell that you come from the south.' What do you call it? The theory of relativity?"

I loved how spirited he was: Messina had met his match. But then I remembered what kind of man he was, and I had to intervene again.

"Fabio, I've already told you that we have to find alternative grazing land for the sheep."

"The sheep can go to hell."

"Please remember that I'm Antonio's wife, and I've got the same power of attorney that you've got. We've got to decide together."

I had hoped that at that point, Messina would have told Fabio that the deal was off. But no: it was too important to him.

The older man leered at me.

"I don't doubt," he said to my nephew, "that you also know how to make this beautiful woman see reason. We'll talk again next week."

"Fine," said Fabio, glaring at me.

"I've got the deposit in cash here, and I don't really want to take it away with me. You can have it. If we don't come to an agreement, you can pay it back to me. But I doubt it'll come

139

to that." Then Messina gave something to Fabio. When he had gone, I wanted to rip Fabio to pieces, but he got there first.

"What were you thinking? We had an agreement! You told me not to touch the fields where the crops are grown, nor the cows, nor any of the other things that uncle oversees in person, and I did what you wanted. So now why are you quibbling over a piece of pasturage?"

"Let me explain —"

"Is it because I want to sell three hectares instead of one? Have you any idea how much money we'll make? What do you know about these kinds of deals? Do you know how much rent you can get from ten villas."

"Can you just shut up for one second? I'm very happy with the deal. What I'm not happy about is the name of your buyer, or should I say your business partner, seeing what you've got in mind!"

"Why don't you like Signor Messina? What have they told you about him?"

"Your mother's never mentioned his name?"

"What's it got to do with my mother? She's been in Bologna since..."

He must have realised something for he went white.

"Sit down Fabio and try and stay calm. What I've got to tell you isn't just local gossip."

He sat down. "Go on."

"He was connected to your father's last case. When he was killed. Vincenzo Messina wanted to frame the person that Alfredo was defending. He had paid a false witness to send an innocent man to prison. You know how the story ends. For years people said that your father was killed on the orders of Messina."

Fabio was silent. I had hoped to see some emotion from him, but all he said was:

"Was Messina ever tried for my father's murder?"

"No, there wasn't any evidence. You should know that there's never any direct evidence in these cases. Someone was paid to make it look like the murder of your father was a robbery gone wrong."

"So basically no one has ever found definitive proof against this man."

"Fabio, don't tell me that you think he's innocent. Can't you see what kind of man he is?"

"Do you really think that gossip that circulated twenty years ago will make me turn my back on a good deal."

I was horrified. He got up, opened the envelope that was on the desk and pulled out so many banknotes that I would never have guessed how much money was in his hand.

"This is the deposit that Vincenzo Messina left me. In cash. Now do you understand how much he trusts me?"

"Fabio, the *Mafiosi* always pay in cash, they don't write cheques! It's dirty money, it'll have come from drugs or something similar."

"It seems to me to be a lot cleaner than the money I usually handle," he replied, pretending to examine the note by rubbing it with his fingertips. How can he joke about such things?

"Think about it, Fabio!"

"I've already thought about it. Half of this money is yours. Take it." He put a couple of wads in my lap.

"What am I going to do with all of this?" I asked, bewildered.

"First of all, buy yourself an evening dress. Dark green. On Saturday, I'll take you to the theatre. Do you like the opera?"

"But —"

"Start spending it. Start to enjoy yourself. Isn't that what you want?"

"Darling,, it's money from a murderer."

"It wasn't your father who was murdered, it was mine. Why

141

should you care where it comes from?"

His words made my blood run cold. Fabio continued: "Be that as it may, don't you want to see the opera? Tomorrow, buy yourself a dark green velvet dress."

"Why does it have to be dark green?" I didn't have the strength to argue.

"Process of elimination. Black annoys me. White makes me think of weddings. Pink reminds me of the fairy in Pinocchio. Red, pink and yellow don't suit blondes. But dark green with your green eyes. Mmmh!"

Nobody had ever cared about what I wore before. I was confused, and he knew it. He kissed me on the neck, whispering: "I can't wait to take the most beautiful lady in Sicily to the theatre."

That's how he managed to silence me, and now I'm in the sitting room regretting the fact that I didn't punch him.

Is it all my fault for having created a monster? I admit I did put a few ideas in his head when he was sixteen. But it's one thing to think about selling inherited land, quite another to arrive at such levels of wickedness.

No, I refuse to accept that it's all my fault. Fabio must have had the seeds already planted inside him; they were all ready there when he threatened his stepfather with a knife.

Who does he get him from? Certainly not from Alfredo, who died fighting for justice, nor from Arianna, whom I shouldn't think badly of. Arianna was no different to all the other women. She only wanted to be happy.

Like me.

October 13th

Something terrible has happened.

I went out with Fabio to get a couple of things in the city, and when we got back we found Antonio waiting for us in the living room: sober and angry.

"Fabio," he said. "I got a phone call today from someone who wanted to speak to you. The secretary of the notarial lawyer, Alessi."

The boy turned pale when he heard the name of the notary who was dealing with the sale of the land. I remained silent, waiting for him to come up with a suitable story.

"What was the name of the notary? I don't understand.," said Fabio.

"Alessi. It seems as if you left a message on his answer machine saying that you needed to have a deed of sale drawn up. What are you selling?"

"Me? Nothing! Uncle, she probably got the wrong number."

"It wasn't the wrong number. The young lady was looking for a Mister Altavilla, that's you isn't it? Your name isn't in the telephone directory, therefore you had to be the one that left a message with the notary's secretary."

"You must have imagined it, Uncle."

"Do you think I'm an idiot?!?!"

"No, not an idiot, just someone who drinks too much."

"That's enough!" shouted Antonio, and I had never heard him shout like that before. "I'm not drunk and I've got a message for you. Everything is perfectly clear. The notary has made you an appointment for Thursday at seven o'clock. Thursday at seven, don't forget. Now tell me what you've got to do there, and what you want to sell!"

At this point I would have preferred to give Antonio a sliver of truth, something about how we were going to sell two thousand metres as a favour to a person who needs the space for another outbuilding. I looked at Fabio. *Why don't you touch on the truth at this point?* I pleaded with my eyes.

But my nephew invented more lies. "Very well Uncle, excuse

me. I wanted to surprise you, but obviously I've failed. I'm not selling, I'm buying something. Do you remember the Picciotto sisters?"

"Yes?"

"They are too old for the farm now, they want to go and live in a retirement home in the city. They're selling their land and it's dirt cheap. It's a real bargain."

Antonio looked bewildered for a moment. "I don't know what to make of —" he murmured, and then, after having thought for a while, said:

"...no, the young lady said you were the seller not the buyer."

"Uncle, I assure you, you've misunderstood."

Then my husband turned to me. "Eva, you and him have the power of attorney. Are you selling a piece of my land? I expect the truth from you."

"We are buying," I said, but without conviction. "But if you aren't happy, we can always cancel the agreement. We'll return the deposit."

It was Fabio who had taught me to lie, but Antonio didn't fall for it.

"Listen to me, both of you. This land has belonged to the Altavillas for three generations. I've written my will and I'm leaving it to you to be used as farmland, not for anything else. You must swear to me that you'll never sell it. I'm leaving it to you, for Fabio's children, for his grandchildren, for all the Altavillas to come! Eva, these heirs should have been born by you. By you, from your womb. I wouldn't be so anxious if you had had at least one child."

I didn't know how to respond, so all I said was:

"Sweetheart, trust Fabio. He's your brother's son."

My words should have calmed Antonio down but instead he looked as if he was about to cry.

"I know," he said. "This is my misfortune."

144

And he set off up the stairs. Off to lock himself in that damn room-cum-shrine to drink, to destroy himself. I could swear he knows.

When I heard the door to the room slam shut, I turned to Fabio and slapped him.

"Ugghh!" he cried, shocked.

"You and that damned Vincenzo Messina! It's gone too far. My husband will die of a broken heart."

I was about to hit him again, but he held my arms. "My dear," he said, in a tone of voice that was anything but affectionate, "don't forget that all this was your idea."

"Yes, but you know full well that you've gone far beyond what I —"

"And never hit me again. You're so beautiful, I wouldn't want to damage such a perfect face. What would I do with a partner who was disfigured?"

He would never hurt me physically, but just arguing with him kills me. He doesn't touch me when we are arguing, and I can't hold out for long without his touch.

I've got to keep quiet. All that I can do now for my husband is remove the alcohol from his room. I wouldn't want his suicide on my conscience too.

December 20th

Tina called to tell me that Mama is very ill. She's got pneumonia and my sister Maria's been helping her, but I'll go this evening and take over. My sisters and brothers have children of their own and they've got to prepare for the festivities, and as I haven't got children, I'm expected to help out over Christmas. I don't mind at all: it'll be nice to spend some time with Mama. She's still very weak but the fever has gone down, so we'll be able to chat a little.

Fabio is being his usual selfish self: he grumbled while I was putting a couple of pairs of clean underwear and a jumper into a bag in preparation for my time away.

"Does this mean," he asked, "that I'll have to spend Christmas alone with a drunkard?"

"You can go out with your friends if you want. You're free to do as you wish."

"I would have preferred to spend Christmas with you."

"I would have liked that too, but it's my mother."

He was silent, angry. If he really does care about me, and if my company is really that important to him, then it's a lot more than I could ever have expected from him. Buoyed by his words, I thought I would ask him to do something for me.

"Please, while I'm gone, try to be nice to your uncle."

"I wasn't aware that I'd ever treated him badly."

"You know full well what I mean. If he has one of his attacks, call me. I'll come at once to give him his injection."

"I can do it. I know what to do."

"I would rather be there. Will you promise me, Fabio?"

"Okay."

I didn't dare tell him that I don't trust him.

December 22nd

Now that I'm with my mother, I wish I were back home. I don't know why. I miss Fabio, and I miss Antonio, or maybe I'm just anxious.

My mother noticed me pacing up and down the room. "Eva, what's wrong?"she said. "Why don't you come and sit down?"

"Nothing. I'm tired of sitting down all the time."

"Problems at home?"

"Just the usual," I replied vaguely.

"Your husband's not well, is he?"

"No."

"Why are you worried about him. He's got his nephew and the paid help looking after him."

"Oh Mama, it's actually his nephew that worries me," I blurted out.

"Why?"

I couldn't tell her everything. I didn't tell her that Fabio was my lover, nor about the three hectares we had sold, but I told her a great deal else that was true: I don't want children, I'll have to share the land with my husband's nephew, his nephew was the type of boy who wanted everything immediately.

"Do you think," said my mother in-between coughing fits, "that Fabio will kill his uncle for his money?"

"No, I don't think so. I don't know. But Antonio is so terribly weak and Fabio won't be looking after him like I do. For example, he won't hide the alcohol."

"I see." She paused. Then she said suddenly, "So it took you four years to fall in love with your husband?"

Her words brought a lump to my throat. "I do love him, but like an old friend," I replied.

"That's a lot more than many wives feel about their husbands."

"Are you serious Mama?"

"Of course. What do you know about marriage? We married you off too young, an 'arranged' marriage, it was a mistake. We didn't give you any time to have other relationships. If you had had the opportunity to experience passion, to love, before you got married, you would have realised that once these feelings fade away, there's nothing left. If you could compare the bond you have with your husband with the transience of love, you'd realise how solid it is."

She was wrong. I should have told her. I know what passion is and it isn't true that it fades away without trace. It burns the soul and nothing will ever grow again on its ashes. A bond cannot be solid with a man who won't let himself be helped, who doesn't trust in his wife, who views her as a breeding machine. I love Antonio but it's with Fabio that I want to spend the rest of my life. Even if I do hate him at times. Yes, I hate him. Is this also passion? What does my mother know about passion? She was married off to a man chosen by her parents too. Is there something in her past that she hasn't told me?

She interpreted my silence as confirmation that I agreed with her and said: "Eva, I don't need help night and day, why don't you go home?"

"You can't be serious."

"Why not? I haven't had a fever for two days now. If my temperature doesn't rise again tonight, I'll only need your father's help. You must return to your husband, if you think he needs you."

"Mama, I promised I would stay here with you until Christmas, and that's what I'm going to do."

"Let the thermometer decide. If the thermometer says I'm out of danger, you can go."

She's a good woman. She's raised seven children but never asks for anything from them, not even a bit of company over Christmas. I pray that her temperature doesn't rise. And I pray to God to help me, even if I don't deserve it. I'm a shameful woman, but I do want to go and see whether Fabio is harming my husband.

I've got a feeling that something terrible is going to happen, and it won't go away. Knives aren't the only way to hurt people.

Antonio's Last Word

December 22nd 1990

They think that I'm always drunk, that I'm so out of it that I don't know they're up to. But I've known what's been going on almost since the beginning.

It didn't take long before I realised that Fabio wasn't like me, that he wouldn't be able to love the farm more than anything else in the world: that I knew the minute Arianna's letter arrived.

I don't reread that letter like I once did, but I've never thrown it away. I look at the envelope every now and then and it still shocks me when I read: 'sender: Arianna Guarneri, via Turati 50.' Not 'Arianna Altavilla,' but the surname she had before she got married. When I saw that surname, that wrong surname, I was filled by such a strong sense of foreboding that I was too scared to open the envelope and I got my wife to do it instead.

"He's got something that makes you drop everything and follow him," Arianna once said of Alfredo. I could never forget those words because I would have said the very same thing. Yet not only has she disowned our surname, she can bear the touch of another man after being touched by Alfredo. The whole thing mystifies me.

When I read that she wanted to turn Fabio into a farmer, well I did believe it for a second: I needed to believe in my nephew as I'd lost everything else. But when I looked into his eyes at the station, I knew I was wrong.

I remember everything about that day. The train was late and I got the strange feeling that this was the second time I was living this moment: the wait for a train that bore a stranger who was destined to turn my life upside down. The first time it was Arianna, this time it was her son, and I call him "stranger" because I hadn't seen him since he was a baby.

I didn't know what type of person he was, but I kept telling myself that it was Alfredo's son so I was bound to like him. He got off the train, elegant and serious, without the *joie di vivre* of boys his age, but with the tired air of one who has already seen what life had to offer. He said: "Are you my Uncle Antonio?" in the voice of a grown man which confused me. It was then that I noticed his eyes: they were blue like Arianna's, but without the sweetness.

Instead of hugging me, he proffered his hand for me to shake and I said something like "What a handsome young man you are," but not even the hint of a smile crossed his face. Why? What had I ever done to him? I, who hadn't drunk for twenty-four hours so I could drive to the station to meet him!

When we got to the car, he said: "Is it far to the farm?"

"Depends on the traffic. Why? Are you in a hurry?"

"No, but if it's going to take more than an hour, I'd better use the toilet at the station."

I said he should go and waited for him there, as still as a statue with his suitcase in my hands. Go to the toilet: what did I expect him to say? Something funny, something profound? Should every word that comes out of his mouth be sublime, just because he's Alfredo's son? What an idiot I was!

He disappointed me twice during his first day here. First off, he preferred to see the city before seeing the farm and then he preferred a bit of cash instead of a horse. It was clear then that he didn't give a damn about the land, but I prayed to God to give me the strength to love him like the son I'd never had. Sometimes I didn't drink so that I would be able to explain how to manage the farmlands, but we were both wasting our time: he couldn't wait to get away from me, and I couldn't wait to drink something; my mouth would be dry from all the talking.

150

I tried to caress him under the chin once, like his father used to do to me when I was his age: what was wrong with that? But Fabio recoiled like a wildcat: it was a miracle he didn't hiss at me.

That evening I got drunk I was so upset, and for the first time I saw strange things: I saw Fabio's eyes on the wall, those eyes that had stared so angrily at me.

Slowly, my faith in that boy crumbled, and I drank more and more, but I never failed to do my duty by Alfredo's son. That's why, when Eva suggested letting him stay with us for a while, maybe forever, I had to agree, even though I could smell the danger. If I hadn't, I would never have had the courage to look at my brother's photo again. When all's said and done, I christened Fabio, I practically brought him up for the first year of his life, and I hoped that one day, he would love me. I would forgive him anything in return for his love.

For a while he had played the part of the good farmer, rising early to help with the milking and such but he didn't have the calling. It finally hit me when I found him sat next to Eva in the sheep pen; they should have been overseeing the shearing, but instead they were telling each other jokes. And in the meantime, a worker had sheared a poor sheep terribly, but Fabio hadn't noticed, hadn't said a word.

But despite all of this, when I had my heart attack, I agreed to sign a power of attorney. Fabio was intelligent, he could always learn new skills, but most importantly he might come to the conclusion that he was better off living in the country than returning to Bologna to his hated stepfather. This is what I really hoped for: that Fabio would change, I didn't care whether he was motivated more by hate for his stepfather than love for the land. He was my heir.

I even feel guilty about the fact that Alfredo would have preferred his son to go to university, an intellectual like he

151

was, while I was trying to awaken a passion for farming in him — Then I remembered that Arianna had a second, horrible husband: You would forgive me, I said to my brother's photo, because after all, he's better off here.

My heart attack sealed my fate. I could have agreed to a limited power of attorney which would have given them the management of the farm for three months or less: there were things to do that couldn't wait, buy a new tractor for example. But a dark force pushed me to agree to give a general power of attorney to a nephew I didn't trust. Why?

I was sober the day the notary came: he had to believe that I had all my wits about me when I signed the power of attorney. But I didn't: there's an alien force inside me that decides these things for me.

It was only when the telephone call arrived about the sale of the land that I realised that I had to stop deluding myself. I had to face up to the truth: Fabio wasn't a son worthy of his father. That day he lied to me, he insulted me, he even told me that I was hallucinating…

I don't know how that story finished: the following Thursday at five o'clock, I should have followed Eva and Fabio, to see where they went…but the usual dark force stopped me once again. I didn't want to know. I wanted to believe that they really buying fields from the Picciotto sisters because I never thought that Eva was capable of lying to me.

She's a real countrywoman like Tina: she likes it here. I remember when she wanted to help with labourers with the grape harvest: her enthusiasm was genuine, not false like the boy's. A woman like Eva doesn't sell land. So why hasn't she realised that Fabio is a liar? She was the one who said: "you've got to trust your brother's son." Something just doesn't add up in all of this.

Maybe they have sold couple of hectares: they're very happy

at the moment; they buy themselves new clothes and go off to the city to have fun. But they could have asked me for money, I've got lots in the bank. And anyway, now they've got the power of attorney, they could have withdrawn it themselves.

The time's arrived for answers. Tonight, December twenty-second. Eva's with her mother so I can confront Fabio without her hearing me. He's shut himself in the downstairs sitting room with a group of rowdy friends that he's invited here to play cards.

I know my nephew's not the sort to forgo the pleasures Christmas brings, but what kind of friends does he have? Each new round of baccarat is heralded by vulgar shrieks. The women are worse than the men, they are screaming like whores and I'm not used to having these kinds of people in my house. Oh, yes, this time Fabio's gone too far: I'll tell him. As soon as he comes out of that room I'll tell him a thing or two.

After a while, he came out into the corridor to show one of his female guests the way to the bathroom. What a horrendous girl, carrot coloured punk hair and a miniskirt in the December chill! Where on earth did he find her? I'm sure he touched her down there as he was showing her the way.

I took advantage of that moment to take Fabio by the arm before he could go back into the sitting room.

"Hey!" he cried. "What do you want Uncle?"

"What do I want? I want to know why you've brought this rabble into my house!"

"It's not like they're thieves or anything. We're only playing cards."

"Are all the girls like the one that I saw a minute ago?"

"What do you care? It isn't a drug den if that's what you're thinking."

"I care because the lady of the house has a mother who is ill and is doing everything she can to help her. She wouldn't want you to be having these kinds of parties while she's not here, and with people from the gutter to boot! As soon as Eva comes home, I'll tell her everything, she won't think you're a saint by the time I've finished."

"You can tell her all you want. You can tell her that the house was full of druggies but the truth is, she'll never believe you. Everyone knows that you see things that don't exist — spiders on the walls, cockroaches on the sofas. Now if you would excuse me, I have to go."

Little rascal. If he has the cheek to talk to me like that, then everything that I've suspected is true. Even the sale of the land.

How I wish that Alfredo and Arianna's son wasn't incapable of loving me, of loving the land, of feeling anything positive about this place. But his betrayal is my fault, I asked to be stabbed in the back and now I know what dark force pushed me into this situation: I had to pay for it someday.

I brought the boy to live with me to atone for what I thought that fateful day, when we were waiting for Alfredo to come home, but he never did.

I wanted Arianna and I had to pay for having thought about her like that. Well, I've finally fulfilled my destiny and paid my debt. The worst possible thing has happened: I'm badly treated and despised by my brother's son.

But it's my debt, it shouldn't fall on my father's land. I'm the one who has to pay. Fabio can take my valuables and lock me up in a care home if he wants, but he can't sell the land! I must tell him. I'll wait until he comes out of that room...

Why has he brought those sluts here? His brother had refined tastes; he would never have done anything like that. He liked those divas with porcelain features…now I remember her name. Kim Novak. He must have passed on his ideal of feminine beauty to me for I married a girl just like her.

Poor Eva. What have I given her? My child bride, my patient

nurse, she's received nothing for the sacrifices she's made.

Eva. I know I could have loved her if I hadn't been so obsessed with the ghosts of the past. What did Arianna have that you haven't got? Why did I fall in love with her?

Oh, now I understand why!

It was because Alfredo said that I cared about his wife and from the moment he said it, it was true.

It's taken me forty years to understand that my brother is the only person I've ever loved…

I've got to talk to Fabio. I can hear one of the girls asking for something to drink, so he's got to leave the room to get the alcohol. I'll stop him when he comes out…

"Fabio, I am absolutely certain. I wasn't hallucinating."

"Uncle, what are you on about?"

"The notary, Alessi. He said that you were selling a piece of land. I want the truth. What did you sell, to whom did you sell it to, and why?"

"It's nothing Uncle, calm down. I sold half a hectare to the guy that buys milk from us. He wants to expand his cheese factory. That's all it was."

"Who is this person?"

"I told you, he's one of our customers. I'm sure you'll have heard of him. Vincenzo Messina. Your five thousand metres squared will stay in the family, if I may say so."

"Vincenzo Messina? Yes, it rings a bell. But it wasn't a cheese factory, no. Something else."

"Why didn't you tell me any of this before?"

"Because I was afraid that you would be against the idea, and I didn't want to lose out on the deal. We made loads of money from the sale, Uncle. Our land was the only land suitable, so Messina paid us way above the odds for half a hectare. You're a good farmer but I'm a good businessman. Trust me."

"Will that money be reinvested in the land? To improve the

155

quality of the livestock?"

"Yes, of course."

"I don't believe you. You've already spent it having fun, or you've gambled it away," I accused him.

His expression hardened. "What are you worried about Uncle? You'll have land as far as the eye can see as long as you're alive."

As long as I'm alive? Well that slipped out!

"Does that mean that when I die, you'll sell all the rest?"

The flash of anger in his eyes tells me that he's tired of lying, tired of wasting time with me while his friends are waiting for him, and I know that if I insist, I'll get the truth out of him.

"What difference does it make? When you're dead you won't care!"

I pull him up by his lapels. "It's my land. It's in my blood!" I shout. "If anything happens, I'll hear about it even if I'm six feet under! You can't sell it! I won't leave it to you if you're going to sell it!"

"Well change your will then. You were sober when you wrote it, but no notary will think you're sober if you were to try to change it now. All those medical certificates that show. Get your hands off my jacket, it cost a shed load of money."

I let him go, shocked. I've only got one more card left to play.

"There are two heirs to this farm. My wife would never let you sell it. She loves the land."

Fabio is laughing. Shit. What's he got to laugh about?

"I know she supported you over that five thousand metres squared, but selling the whole farmstead is a different matter. Eva would never agree, never," I say.

"But it was her idea in the first place!"

"What? No you'll never make me believe that's true."

"Wake up, Uncle. Your wife is a twenty four year old girl

156

who's never seen anything but fields and cows. She wants to travel, see new places. I think I'll take her on a cruise next summer."

"On a cruise? Are you mad? You and your aunt? People would say it was improper. Eva would never agree."

"Come to think of it, we've done a lot that you could call improper!"

While I'm trying to come to terms with what he was telling me, for hearing the truth was like a lightening bolt had hit my brain, out of the sitting room comes that horrendous girl with the carrot coloured hair.

"Fabio," she says, "what the hell are you doing? We're all waiting for you."

"Sorry, it's my Uncle's fault. I can't tell him to get out, he's still the head of this house. But he won't be for much longer."

The girl laughs like a goose and goes back into the sitting room.

"You — and Eva? I don't believe it. Fabio, I maybe a drunk and I maybe stupid but I know my wife. You're lying."

"It's true that I have lied about some things but I would never hurt Eva. I owe a lot to her. But you Uncle should have a good look at your conscience. What have you ever given her in four years of marriage? Should she be grateful that at least you did her when she was fertile?"

He knows that too? It's all true. It's all my fault. As I didn't give her any love, she turned to this delinquent. Now I believe him.

"So is it all decided then? You're just waiting until I die?"

Fabio didn't reply.

"Are you going to marry her? Do you intend to marry her and make her happy like I never knew how to? Or are you going to cheat on her with every whore you come across like that slag who's waiting for you in the living room?"

"Nice. You're worried about the fate of a wife who cheated on you? It would be enough to make me believe that you were madly in love with her if I didn't know that you've spent your life in love with another woman!"

He knows that too. Oh God, I don't feel well. He even knows about Arianna, that's why he's always so sure of himself.

His uncle, that wretch, could never have stopped him. My head's spinning.

"Fabioooo!" someone shouts from the living room. "Where have the drinks got to?"

"Coming..." He turns towards the living room, but I follow him.

"Fabio, wait. I just want you to promise me one thing: don't sell the land. Do what you want with me, lock me away in a home, hand the farm over to a tenant farmer and go off and enjoy yourselves as you wish. At least give me that."

In the living room he opens the china cabinet. That's where Eva has hidden the alcohol. She did it for me, for my own good.

"Fabio, are you listening to me? I would do anything to save my land. It was my only reason for living after your father died, otherwise I would have shot myself with my hunting rifle. Seeing that you know everything, you should know that too. It was my love for this land that gave me the strength to carry on..."

He's not listening to me. He looks at me without saying a word, takes two bottles, and goes back into the living room.

Poor Eva. She did care about me once, but I can't blame her for falling for Fabio. He's a master in the art of seduction, just as his father was. Only in that respect is he his father's son.

Eva my child, why don't you come home? I've got to warn you about Fabio. He's using you and he'll cast you aside like an old shoe once you have sold the land. I've got to talk to you immediately...

I've got to have a drink. A drink, my throat's burning.

Ahah. I know where the alcohol is kept. Fabio didn't take all of it for his friends. He's left the brandy. There's some brandy in the cabinet. I'll make do with the brandy.

Hell, the glass won't keep still. Or is it my hands….

Now it's my stomach that's burning, but it is a nice feeling. It'll warm me up. I must phone Eva, I must tell her to come home.

The telephone's never in the same place. What's the number for Eva's mother?

Five, seven, busy. Hell, the line's busy. The brandy's taking effect, in fifteen minutes or so I'll have forgotten that I have to call her.

Eva, why can't you hear my thoughts? Why doesn't your heart hear me calling you? Eva, come home...

Little one, I'm not angry with you. I got what I deserved...

I've got to calm down, I've got to take my tranquillisers, they'll work better with the alcohol. Where have I put them?

Of course, they're in my room. I've got to go upstairs. How odd, the steps are twisted, it would be so easy to fall.

Here are my pills. Ants? How did ants get into the box, on the first floor?

No, they aren't ants. I mustn't forget that they're a figment of my imagination. It's just not that easy to grab a pill in the midst of all those ants...

Got it! Now I'll be able to sleep. I just want a quick word with Alfredo before I do.

Alfredo, your candle's almost burnt down to the wick. It might last a few more hours, but if I fall asleep, I won't wake up in time to replace it: best do it now. You must never be without a lit candle.

Where have I put the new ones? I can't remember. Damn,

why do I always forget everything?

For example, what was the name of that person Fabio was talking about? Giovanni Messina. Have I met him before?

Who knows if he will be the one who will buy the land when I die. I mustn't think about it, I've still got time to persuade her not to do it!

Alfredo, you know everything, don't you? You can forgive me now. I've paid my debt. Your son is taking away all the things that I love and he'll destroy them. I couldn't have been given a worse punishment.

Alfredo, tell me that you've forgiven me. Tell me with your eyes: I'll read it in your eyes.

Look at me. Yes. You've forgiven me. I'm at peace now. At peace because nothing more can happen to me.

Brandy and pills, I won't be able to move soon. I must replace the candle.

Now I remember: the new candles are in the cupboard in the study, downstairs. I've got to go back downstairs.

Okay, that's the first step without falling. One…two…why are they twisted?

How come there's only one candle in the cupboard? I bought loads….but it's just full of papers. Alfredo's papers, lawyer stuff. Why are they still here after twenty years?

Let's see what's in them. *There's no evidence that Vincenzo Collura killed…*

Now I remember: these are the documents about the last case. The last one. I've always kept them out because I've never considered the case closed; I've always thought that one day someone would have taken those papers to avenge Alfredo's death…

He's been waiting for someone to avenge his death for nineteen years, and if I had filed those papers away, it would have been like admitting defeat. But it's not over yet, and I won't throw those papers away. The judges may think that the case is closed, but I don't...

There is no evidence to suggest that Vincenzo Collura killed Giuseppe Messina. The charge was brought based on unreliable evidence from Calogero Sardo and I will now tell you about his past criminal history so that you may judge if...

Hang on a minute. Giuseppe Messina was dead. It was his brother who paid the false witnesses, he was called...

Vincenzo Messina!

Oh God, that's the man Fabio was talking about, he is...

My land! Not to him! No! No!

I don't feel well, everything is black. Black.

Where am I?

I'm in bed. How long have I slept? Somebody must have put me to bed, I was...

Oh, Eva's here. She must have heard my call and come back. Damn, I can't remember what I had to say to her.

She's holding my hand and crying. She's saying something. What's she saying?

"Antonio! Antonio, are you awake? Don't go back to sleep! Hang in there. I've called an ambulance. It's been held up by the Christmas traffic, but it's on its way. Hang in there my love, don't leave me! Can you hear me? Can you hear me?"

Yes. I can hear her.

"Listen to me. I decided to come home to surprise you and I found you collapsed in the study while Fabio was partying in the other room, and he hadn't even noticed. Nobody had tried to help you! Oh, my love, it won't happen again, I promise. I've kicked Fabio and all his terrible friends out. I've thrown them out, do you understand me?"

I can hear you Eva. I can't speak but I can hear what you're saying.

161

Something's coming back to me. You can't kick Fabio out because soon I'll be dead and he'll be the master of this house. If you're not careful, he'll become your *master too. I want to tell you, but I can't find my voice.*

"I told him to spend the night at the house of one of his sluts! What has he done to you? Antonio, my love, what has he done to you?"

Is she crying? No one's ever cried for me before. Isn't she sweet with her little blonde head resting on my arm.

I would like to stroke it, but I can't move. How odd. I was convinced I had lifted by arm up, but it's still on the floor.

"Antonio! Oh God, he's not breathing! Doctor, he's not breathing!"

I'm not breathing but I can still hear you. You loved me Eva. Only you.